An Explosive Finish

Joe gunned the throttle and zipped over the hill, catching a bit of air as he did so. He didn't try anything fancy, wanting to get a feel for the course first. His steady progress put him in third place, behind the two leaders. He spotted Frank, watching from beyond the next rise, then lost sight of him as he hit the ground again.

Hawk topped the next hill before Henderson. She did a barhop over her handlebars as she went, then disappeared behind the hill.

Henderson topped the next rise, gunning his throttle all the way as he went up. He hit the top of the whoopdedoo in a nearly vertical climb and twisted his bike into the first somersault in a combination.

Man and machine hung gracefully in the air for a moment—then Henderson's black and gold motorcycle exploded.

The Hardy Boys Mystery Stories

#109 The Prime-Time Crime
#110 The Secret of Sigma Seven
#139 The Search for the Snow Leopard
#140 Slam Dunk Sabotage
#141 The Desert Thieves
#143 The Giant Rat of Sumatra
#152 Danger in the Extreme
#153 Eye on Crime
#154 The Caribbean Cruise Caper
#156 A Will to Survive
#159 Daredevils
#160 A Game Called Chaos
#161 Training for Trouble
#162 The End of the Trail
#163 The Spy That Never Lies
#164 Skin & Bones
#165 Crime in the Cards
#166 Past and Present Danger
#167 Trouble Times Two
#168 The Castle Conundrum
#169 Ghost of a Chance
#170 Kickoff to Danger

#171 The Test Case
#172 Trouble in Warp Space
#173 Speed Times Five
#174 Hide-and-Sneak
#175 Trick-or-Trouble
#176 In Plane Sight
#177 The Case of the Psychic's Vision
#178 The Mystery of the Black Rhino
#179 Passport to Danger
#180 Typhoon Island
#181 Double Jeopardy
#182 The Secret of the Soldier's Gold
#183 Warehouse Rumble
#184 The Dangerous Transmission
#185 Wreck and Roll
#186 Hidden Mountain
#187 No Way Out
#188 Farming Fear
#189 One False Step
#190 Motocross Madness
The Hardy Boys Ghost Stories

Available from ALADDIN Paperbacks

HARDY BOYS®

#190

MOTOCROSS MADNESS

FRANKLIN W. DIXON

Aladdin Paperbacks
New York London Toronto Sydney

First Aladdin Paperbacks edition April 2005
Copyright © 2005 by Simon & Schuster, Inc.

ALADDIN PAPERBACKS
An imprint of Simon & Schuster
Children's Publishing Division
1230 Avenue of the Americas
New York, NY 10020

The text of this book was set in New Caledonia.

Printed in the United States of America
2 4 6 8 10 9 7 5 3 1

THE HARDY BOYS MYSTERY STORIES is a trademark of Simon & Schuster, Inc.

THE HARDY BOYS and colophon are registered trademarks of Simon & Schuster, Inc.

Library of Congress Control Number 2004106922

ISBN 0-689-87365-4

Contents

1	Race for Life	1
2	Bird of Prey	10
3	The Kick-start Party	21
4	Where There's Smoke . . .	34
5	Down & Dirty	46
6	Flameout	57
7	Thousands to One	67
8	Wiped Out	78
9	Off Course	88
10	Down & Out	98
11	Endurance	107
12	Hidden Dangers	118
13	Not Out of the Woods Yet	126
14	A Long Way Down	134
15	The Great Plan	142

1 Race for Life

"Yeah! Way to go, Jamal!" Joe called.

Jamal Hawkins skidded his dirt bike to a halt at the corner of the track, kicking up a huge cloud of tawny dust. Several other racers, clad in colorful motocross "armor," zoomed by as Jamal pulled up next to his friends, Joe and Frank Hardy.

Joe, a muscular, blond seventeen-year-old, clapped Jamal on the shoulder. "Nice bit of riding," he said.

Joe's older brother, Frank, checked his stopwatch and nodded in agreement. "Good run."

"How good?" Jamal asked. He flipped up the faceplate of his motorcycle helmet and mopped his brow. His brown face glistened in the afternoon sunlight. It was sweaty work keeping a motocross bike under control over the rough course at the Fernandez Cycle Track. The raceway, located near the western outskirts of Bayport, was a long, unpaved series of hills, twists, and cutbacks.

Frank showed Jamal his lap time. "A few seconds under your previous track record," the elder Hardy said. "Not bad for the first run of the day."

Jamal pulled off his red and black helmet and smiled. "You guys ain't seen nothing yet," he said. "I'm saving my best stuff for the Rehab Race this weekend. You guys should take a shot at it too. It's open to everyone."

"We've done our share of rough riding over the years," Frank said, "but I doubt our bikes are up to that kind of competition. They're really just recreation bikes, not racing models."

"Hey, I've heard that it's the *rider* that wins the day, not the machine," Joe said playfully.

"That might be true if all the competitors were running 125 cc engines," Frank said. "But facing our little off-roaders against one of those big 250s or 500s . . . well, let's just say that I don't like eating that much dust." He brushed the grit that Jamal's bike had kicked up out of his dark hair.

"But I'm riding my 125 too," Jamal said. He patted the gas tank of his red and black machine. "All the competitors are doing the same. The Fernandez family has limited the entries to small

2

bikes so that more people will join the fund-raiser."

"That's right," a pleasant female voice interjected. "We—or at least *I*—need as many competitors in this race series as I can get."

The Hardys and their friend turned and saw a teenager with wavy blond hair coming toward them. She smiled and looked very upbeat, even though she was seated in a wheelchair. She rolled skillfully over the packed earth at the edge of the motocross track.

"Hi, Corri," Jamal said. "Guys, this is Corrine Fernandez. Corrine, these are my friends, Frank and Joe Hardy."

Joe and Frank shook hands with the girl. "Isn't this benefit race being held in your honor?" Frank asked.

Corrine nodded. "I don't know if I'd call it an 'honor,' but . . . my dad and the rest of the family put this together to help cover my rehab bills. I wanted to call it the 'Race to Avoid Bankruptcy,' but they decided to go with the 'Corrine Fernandez Benefit Challenge' instead." She chuckled.

Frank smiled. "That's probably easier to sell to the media than your other option."

"Well," Corri said, "with the popularity of reality TV right now, we might do better if we called it 'Death Race 3000.'"

Jamal and the Hardys all laughed.

"How are you feeling?" Joe asked Corrine. "We read about your accident in the papers."

"That was six months ago now," she said, "and I'm still in this darn chair." She sighed. "I can't wait to get back on a bike again." She looked wistfully at the colorful riders practicing on the track nearby.

"So you're planning to race again?" Frank asked.

"You bet," Corrine replied. "When you fall off the bike, you've gotta get right back on."

"Not when you fall off, break both legs, and fracture your spine in three places," Jamal said.

Corri shrugged. "Hey, we're a motocross family. Racing's in our blood."

"Just so long as that blood doesn't end up on the track," Joe said.

"Don't worry," Corrine replied. "I just caught a bad break. Motocross isn't that dangerous if you know what you're doing."

"She's right," Jamal said cheerily. "I doubt I've broken more than a couple bones in all the time I've been doing it."

"If you've only broken two bones, maybe you're not doing it right," Joe quipped.

"If fractures are your idea of 'right,' maybe it's a good thing that you don't race as much as I do, Joe," Jamal replied.

Corrine laughed. "Boy, do I miss the repartee of the track!" she said. "I'm getting stronger every day, though. I'm sure I'll be zooming over whoopde-doos in no time."

"Your family owns this track, don't they?" Frank asked.

"Yes," Corrine said. "For now, anyway. Dad had to sell the mortgage to cover my medical bills. He's wishing now that we had better health insurance, but . . ." She shrugged again, then asked the Hardys, "So, are you two going to join the field, or what?"

"We were just telling Jamal that our bikes might not be up to the challenge," Frank said.

"You can do it," Corri said. "This series of races will give everyone a chance to win—even talented amateurs. The bike engine size is limited to 125 cc, though you're allowed minor modifications after every phase of the race. The winner will be the rider who does best in all three parts of the event."

"What are the three phases?" Frank asked.

"I can answer that," Jamal said. "There's the acrobatic/aerobatic Mixed Freestyle, the motocross Speed Test, and finally, the cross-country Enduro."

"The winner of the series will get a rebuilt classic O'Sullivan SD5—an offshoot of the old BSA line of British machines," Corrine said.

"Is it worth much?" Joe asked.

"It's not as rare as an Indian bike," Jamal said, "but it's still a nice piece of iron. And some of the parts came from the garage of motocross legend Garth Metzger."

"I've heard of him," Frank said. "That's quite a prize."

"I'm surprised you can't sell it to cover the bills," Joe said.

"It'd be worth a lot more if the *whole* bike came from Metzger's garage," Corrine admitted. "But it's still a nice collector's item. It's one of a kind. Plus, owning it will mean you're the winner of the most unique motocross race series, ever."

Frank nodded appreciatively. "So, a unique set of races with a unique prize . . . that's one way to get more publicity—and riders—for the race! I hope it works for you."

"So far, so good," Corrine said. "We've got a good mix of amateurs and big-name talent."

"I've heard that Ed Henderson and Amber Hawk will be competing," Joe said. "Even with the unusual format, do you really think local riders have any chance against those two?"

"They're only experts in one type of motocross racing," Jamal said. "Henderson is the king of acrobatics, and Hawk rules on the dirt track. Here, they'll have to compete in specialties they're not used to."

"And on bikes a lot smaller than the ones they normally ride," Corri added. "It wouldn't surprise me if a complete unknown wins the top prize this weekend."

"I guess we'd fit into the 'complete unknown' category," Frank noted.

Corrine smiled up at him and Joe. "So, what do you say, guys? Will you help out and join the race? You could be pledge racers—just like most of the competitors."

"What's a pledge racer?" Joe asked.

"It's like working on a school fund-raiser," Corri explained. "You promise to race, and then collect money by getting people to sponsor you. They pledge either a set amount, or an amount based on where you finish in the standings, or both."

"That's what I'm doing," Jamal added. "There are a lot of people who'll be paying off big-time when I collect that O'Sullivan SD5." He grinned from ear to ear.

"You don't have to ask for huge amounts of money, though," Corrine continued. "Every little bit will help pay for my rehab. The doctors don't care if they're paid in pennies or hundred-dollar bills."

"Well, when you put it that way," Joe said, "how can we refuse?"

"Count us in," Frank agreed.

"Great," Corri said, smiling. She opened a metal clipboard on her lap. "It just so happens that I have a couple of registration forms with me. If you're quick, you might even get in some practice runs today."

"Speaking of practice," Jamal said, "I'd better get back on the course. I hear I've got two more tough competitors entering the race."

Jamal pulled his helmet back on, started the

cycle's engine, and pulled out onto the track once more. "See you after the next run," he called.

Frank started the lap counter on his stopwatch. Then both he and Joe took the registration forms from Corri Fernandez and began filling them out.

While the brothers wrote, they kept an eye on the other racers flying around the track. Clouds of dust whipped up as the dirt bikes crested the hills—known as "whoopdedoos"—and then skidded into the turns between. The sounds of racing engines and the smell of motor fuel mixed with the rich scent of freshly turned earth.

"Those are pretty large whoopdedoos, aren't they?" Frank asked.

"Yeah," Corri said, gazing longingly at the racers. "We've built them up so people can practice for tomorrow's acrobatic event," she said. "We're going to make them even higher overnight, then take them back down for the regular motocross."

A rider in blue racing armor crested the nearest hill. A golden dragon motif covered the painted portion of his bike. As he topped the rise, he flew into the air. He and the bike executed a double somersault, then landed lightly on the track below. The rider kept going, full speed.

Joe and Frank both stopped filling out their forms long enough to watch. "Impressive," Joe finally said.

"That's Ed Henderson," Corri explained. "He's definitely one of the best in the business."

"Don't be looking for jumps like that from us," Frank said, smiling. "Not unless you're providing stunt doubles."

Corrine smiled back. "I think you Hardys protest too much," she said. "Jamal's told me you're pretty fancy riders yourselves."

"Maybe we just want the competition to *think* we're inexperienced," Joe suggested with a laugh.

"It wouldn't be the first time someone's tried that tactic," Corri said. She watched as Henderson zoomed over another rise, then disappeared behind a bank as he continued running the course.

The roar of another engine made all three teens look back the other way.

A pink and purple bike sailed over the crest of the nearby hill. But the rider hit the jump wrong and veered sharply off the track.

"Look out!" Frank shouted as the motorcycle soared right toward them.

2 Bird of Prey

The world seemed to move in slow motion as the cycle flew through the air at the startled teens.

Instinctively, Joe and Frank both grabbed Corrine's wheelchair. They pushed her aside and dove out of the way as the machine zoomed at them. The pink and purple bike rocketed past, missing the brothers by inches.

Corri pitched forward and almost tumbled out of her chair, just managing to hold on. Joe and Frank landed hard in the mud beside the racetrack. The cyclist hit the dirt at an angle and skidded sideways. Her wheels went out from under her, and she crashed into several bales of hay lining the side of the course.

Joe and Frank glanced at Corrine, who looked

pretty shook up. "Are you all right?" Joe asked.

Corri nodded, and ran one shaky hand through her tousled hair.

The brothers rose and headed toward the cyclist. She was lying prone beneath her pink and purple bike, covered with smashed hay. For a moment, she didn't move. Then she groaned and pushed weakly at the cycle, which was pinning her left leg.

Frank and Joe raced to her side and helped lift the machine.

"I'll be all right," the pink-helmeted cyclist said. "The hay bales cushioned the crash. Thank heaven for body armor, too." The brothers noticed that she had motocross impact plates woven into her pink and purple cycling outfit.

At that moment, another bike crested the jump hill. Its rider wore green, with a yellow bird motif painted on her cycle. She paused just a moment, then kept going.

The crashed cyclist snarled, "Amber Hawk . . . !"

"You should take it easy," Joe suggested.

The young woman pulled off her helmet, revealing a pretty face surrounded by dark, wavy hair. "I'm okay," she said.

"That was a pretty bad crash," Frank noted. "You should keep still until we can call for an ambulance."

The woman shook her head. "No need. I've been in worse spills. But thanks for helping. Who are you guys, anyway? Are you part of the staff?"

"Frank and Joe Hardy," Frank replied. "We're signing up for the race and just happened to be here."

"In the right place at the right time," the woman said. "I'm Marissa Hayday."

"Are you all okay?" Corri Fernandez asked. It had taken her some time to wheel across the rutted course shoulder to the scene of the accident.

"Yeah. We're fine," Joe said. "It was a close call, though."

Corri looked very concerned. "What happened?"

Before Marissa could answer, two men came running up to the group. They were both tall and dark-haired. One was younger, about the same age as Corrine. The other man was older, and wore glasses and a bushy mustache. Both bore a family resemblance to Corri.

"We saw what happened," the younger man blurted.

"Corri, are you all right?" the older man asked. "If anything else happened to you—"

"I'm fine, Pops," Corri said.

"I thought for sure that bike was going to clock you," the younger man said. He glared angrily at Marissa Hayday.

"My friends pushed me out of the way in time," Corri explained. "Dad, Paco, this is Joe and Frank Hardy. They're entering the race. Frank, Joe, this is my dad, Peter, and my brother, Paco."

"Pleased to meet you," Joe and Frank said.

The Fernandez men nodded acknowledgment but remained focused on the battered motorcycle rider and her bike. Marissa straightened the machine out and began checking it for damage.

"You could have killed someone, you know," Paco said angrily.

"This is only a practice," Pops added. "You shouldn't be taking those kinds of chances."

"Don't tell *me*," Marissa replied. "Tell that Hawk woman. She's the one who ran me off the course!"

"Amber Hawk?" Pops asked.

"Who else?" Marissa said angrily.

Paco grimaced. "I told you she was trouble, Pops," he said. "We never should have invited her. We ought to kick her out of the competition right now!"

"You think I should throw out one of the best motocross riders on the word of this girl?" Pops asked skeptically.

"Look," Marissa said, "I know I'm nobody important, but I'm telling the truth. Ask my sisters Elena and Kari if you don't believe me. They saw the whole thing."

"Maybe you should flag Hawk down and ask her what happened," Frank suggested.

"Good idea," Pops said. He pulled a small walkie-talkie from his belt and called one of his assistants. A few moments later, he turned back to the group. "I called Stephenson up in the observation tower.

He'll flag down Hawk and send her over. Now, you're sure you're all right, Corrine?"

"Yeah, I'm okay," Corri said.

Jamal's red and black bike crested the nearby hill. He came downslope and stopped near his friends. "How'd I do?" he asked, looking at Frank and Joe.

"Sorry, Jamal," Frank said. He pulled the watch out of his pocket, but his dive had made it reset itself. "We had some trouble here. I completely lost track of your lap time."

"What happened?" Jamal asked, concerned.

"Ms. Hayday nearly plowed into us," Joe offered.

"It wasn't my fault," Marissa said.

"Not your fault, how?" Jamal asked.

"That's what we're trying to determine," Pops replied.

"Everyone's okay, though," Corri added. "That's what's important."

A moment later, a green and yellow bike topped the hill. It skidded to a halt beside the group. Amber Hawk pulled off her helmet and looked at the Fernandez family. "They told me you wanted to see me," she said. "What about?"

"We want to find out what happened when Ms. Hayday here almost crashed," Pops explained.

Hawk shrugged. "What's to know?" she said. "The girl can't handle her bike."

"That's not true!" Marissa protested. "You practically plowed into me."

"Tough competition is part of the game," Hawk replied. "If you don't like the heat, get out of the kitchen."

"Maybe I will," Marissa shot back.

"Now, now," Pops said. "No need to do anything hasty. This is just a misunderstanding." Paco didn't say anything, but stood fuming near his father.

"You should take it easy during these practice runs, Ms. Hawk," Corrine said. "Save something for the actual races."

Amber Hawk sneered. "I've got *plenty* for race day," she said. "Just keep the amateurs out of my way." She pulled her helmet back on, revved her engine, and roared away.

"Nice girl," Joe said, meaning just the opposite.

"We should throw her out of the race," Paco said angrily.

"We can't afford to," Pops replied. "She's one of our biggest draws."

"But everyone *knows* she's a troublemaker," Paco countered.

"Well, she's made enough trouble for me," Marissa Hayday said. "My sisters and I are out of here." Her bike wouldn't start, so she began walking it off the course.

"Paco, go after her," Corri said. "We need all the racers we can get."

"But I *agree* with her," Paco said. "Hawk is a menace."

"Do as your sister asked," Pops said. "She's right. We can't have people dropping out the day before the competition starts. Marissa and her sisters have a lot of supporters."

Paco shot an angry glance at his sister and his father, then jogged off after Marissa.

"Sorry about this," Pops said to the Hardys and Jamal. "We don't usually have these kinds of troubles at our racecourse."

"Everyone's on edge," Jamal said. "Don't worry about it. My friends and I are still in. Aren't we, guys."

Frank and Joe nodded. "We wouldn't miss it," Frank said.

"We've got to finish filling out our entry forms first, though," Joe noted. He looked around and found their papers in the mud nearby. They'd dropped them pushing Corri out of the way of the onrushing motorcycle. "They're ruined, I'm afraid," he said.

Corri glanced at her clipboard, also in the mud nearby. "I'm out too," she said. Jamal picked up the clipboard, dusted it off, and handed it to her. She took the ruined blank forms and threw them into a nearby trash can.

"No problem," Pops said. "I've got plenty of forms in the office. Mr. Hawkins, if you'll take my daughter to the medical center, I'll see to your friends."

"But, Pops," Corrine said, "I'm okay. Really."

Jamal smiled at her. "I promise to get you back on the racecourse in short order," he said.

The wheelchair-bound girl smiled back. "I'll hold you to that promise, Hawkins," she said. Jamal parked his bike out of the way, then wheeled Corri toward the medical center—a small, corrugated metal office near the track's starting line.

As the sun set, Peter Fernandez watched his daughter go. A mixture of admiration and concern washed over his craggy face.

"All this must be tough for you," Frank said.

Mr. Fernandez nodded. "It's been difficult since Corri's accident," he admitted. "Our insurance just wasn't enough to cover both her surgery and her rehab. But we're not about to give up now, not when she's so close to recovery."

"I'm sure the race series will raise the money you need," Joe said.

"I hope so," Mr. Fernandez replied. He walked toward the office, a wide trailer home parked near the eastern perimeter of the property. The Hardys went with him.

"Organizing this benefit has been a lot harder than I thought it would be," he continued. "There

17

are some tricky legalities—especially with the big-name racers."

"Like what?" Joe asked as they walked past a line of garages. The buildings looked something like a long storage unit, with individual repair bays set up for each group of race teams.

"Well, the famous ones want to control their image," Mr. Fernandez said. "And their publicity, too. They bring in sponsors, but they make a lot of demands as well. Setting everything up has cost a lot more money than I thought it would."

"But not enough that you could have completed Corri's rehab with that money instead?" Frank asked.

Mr. Fernandez shook his head. "Not nearly enough," he replied. "You know what they say: You have to spend money to make money. I just hope that the money we make is enough."

"We'll do our best to help," Frank said.

Mr. Fernandez smiled at the brothers. "Thanks," he said. "We appreciate that. We appreciate everyone who's spent their time and energy to help Corri out."

They reached the old trailer that rested atop cement blocks next to the chain-link fence that ran around three sides of the property. The fence separated the track from wilderness on the north side and an industrial park on the east. It enclosed everything in the complex except the racecourse itself, which stretched into the wooded hills behind the main property. Twilight was rapidly descending, and long, dark shadows loomed over the grounds. The office was dark inside, too.

Mr. Fernandez took out his keys and grasped the doorknob. The door swung open in his hand. "That's funny," he said to the brothers. "I'd swear I locked it."

As he spoke, the Hardys spotted someone lurking inside the darkened office.

"Someone's in there," Joe whispered.

"What?" Mr. Fernandez said, momentarily confused.

"Keep quiet," Frank cautioned. "Maybe we can take whoever it is by surprise."

"It's probably just Paco," Mr. Fernandez replied.

"Rummaging around in your office with the lights off?" Joe asked.

"Do you really think he had time to get back here after talking to Marissa?" Frank added.

A look of deep concern drew over Mr. Fernandez's face.

"Do you have anything valuable in the office?" Joe asked.

"Not much," Pops whispered back. "Some money and papers in the safe. Do you think we should call the police?"

"It'd be pretty embarrassing if it *does* just turn out to be your son," Joe said.

"Let's take a look," Frank agreed.

The brothers cautiously opened the door and

peered into the darkened office. At the far side of the room, a man with a flashlight was rummaging through some papers. The Hardys had no chance of recognizing him, as he wore leather riding gear and a motorcycle helmet. Black leather gloves covered his hands, and the helmet obscured his face.

Joe took a tentative step inside the room, but a floorboard creaked beneath his foot.

The helmeted man spun and charged toward them.

3 The Kick-start Party

Surprised, Joe stepped back, right into Frank. The helmeted man shoved the off-balance teens, and both brothers tumbled to the floor. Then the intruder kept going.

He pushed past Mr. Fernandez, who stumbled down the short stairs in front of the trailer and landed in a heap on the ground. The helmeted man ran off into the gathering darkness.

Joe and Frank scrambled to their feet and gave chase.

"Are you okay?" Frank called to Mr. Fernandez as they ran.

The older man nodded and puffed, "Yeah."

"Call the cops!" Joe shouted back to him.

The helmeted man ducked around a tall gravel

pile and between two locked metal sheds. The brothers followed.

The intruder, still a good distance ahead of them, headed toward a battered motorcycle parked near the edge of a dirt path.

"If he reaches that cycle," Joe said, "we'll never catch him!"

"Too late!" Frank replied.

The helmeted man jumped on his cycle and kicked the starter. The brothers kept running, hoping they might catch the intruder before the helmeted man could get going, but then they heard the first kick of the engine.

The bandit opened the throttle, and the bike's back tire kicked up a cloud of dirt. The brothers made one last, desperate sprint, but the intruder zoomed away into the darkness.

"Rats!" Joe blurted. "Do you have any idea who he was?"

Frank shook his head. "I couldn't see his face under the mask. The bulky leather jacket hid his build pretty well, too. For all we know, it might even have been a woman under that outfit."

"Well, whoever it was, they knew their way around that old bike," Joe said. "I don't think I could have gotten it going faster with an electric starter."

"Come on," Frank said. "Let's get back to the office. Maybe Mr. Fernandez noticed something that we didn't."

"Let's hope," Joe agreed.

The brothers caught their breath as they walked back to the trailer, which served as the course headquarters. Inside, they found Peter Fernandez sorting through the scattered papers on the floor. Corrine's father looked up hopefully as the Hardys came in.

"Well?" he asked. "Did you catch him?"

Frank and Joe both shook their heads. "He got to a cycle and rode away."

"What are those papers?" Joe asked.

"Just registration forms, mostly," Mr. Fernandez said. "I don't see what use they'd be to anyone."

Frank frowned. "Are the ownership papers for the SD5 in there?"

"Nope," said Mr. Fernandez. "There are some papers about the bike's history, but not the ownership papers. I checked, and those are still safely locked away."

"So the burglar didn't touch the safe," Joe said.

"Apparently not," Mr. Fernandez replied. "It's not the best safe in the world, but maybe this guy wasn't a very good burglar."

"If it was a *guy* at all," Frank said. "Neither of us got a very good look at him. Did you?"

Mr. Fernandez shook his head. "Can't say I did. Are you boys thinking a girl might have done this?"

"We can't rule it out," Joe replied.

The brothers took a few moments to help Mr.

Fernandez straighten out the office. They gathered up the papers and sorted things as best they could.

Finally, Mr. Fernandez said, "That's enough for now. I'll have to sort the rest myself or I'll never find anything again. I have a rather . . . *unique* filing system." He smiled weakly. "Plus, I imagine you boys want to get out of here."

"It's no trouble, really," Frank said.

"Don't worry about it," Mr. Fernandez said, "Just let me find those applications for you. . . ." He rummaged through a pile of papers and pulled out some applications to replace the ones that had gotten ruined earlier.

Joe and Frank filled out the forms. Then Mr. Fernandez certified them, and gave the brothers their contestant numbers and information packets.

"Of course the most important part is the pledge form," Mr. Fernandez said. "I know it's pretty late for you boys to find sponsors, but just do the best you can."

"We've got a pretty good network of friends and relatives," Frank said.

"We'll come through for you," Joe added. "Good night, Mr. Fernandez."

"Oh! I almost forgot," Mr. Fernandez said. "There's a big kick-start party tonight for the contestants. There'll be food and drinks, and we hope a lot of media will be coming to cover the benefit. I hope you two will be able to come. Bring some friends, if you like."

"Sure thing," Joe said.

"The party's being held at the Veterans of Foreign Wars Memorial Hall, just down the street," Pops added. "The VFW was nice enough to donate their place to use for our cause. You'll find information about the party in your contestant packet. It'll be a good chance to check out our grand prize—as well as the other competitors. The bike will be on display during the festivities."

"I wouldn't mind having a classic motorcycle," Frank said.

Joe winked at Mr. Fernandez. "He'll have to beat *me* to get it, though."

They all laughed, and the brothers headed out. As they left they passed the police, who were coming to take a report on the break-in. The Hardys found Jamal, who'd gotten back from his errand with Corri, near the gate.

"How's she doing?" Joe asked.

"Right as rain," Jamal said. "You'd never know she nearly got clobbered by a runaway motorcycle."

"It's amazing that she maintains such a positive attitude, despite the wheelchair," Frank said.

"I guess you can overcome any obstacle if you put your mind to it," Joe added.

"She was like that in school, too," Jamal said. "I

had a couple of classes with her before she graduated. Corri's one tough cookie. The way she's going, I'm sure she'll get out of that chair one day. All she needs is the money. We can't let her down."

"Don't worry," Frank said. "We'll gather as many pledges as we can."

"Speaking of which," Joe said, "we need to get home and start making calls."

"Will I see you at the kick-start party later?" Jamal asked.

"Definitely," Frank said.

"We might even bring Iola and Callie with us," Joe said. "If they're not tied up. You know how busy our girlfriends' schedules can be."

The three friends went their separate ways, and the Hardys drove home in their van.

That night, the brothers worked the phones, lining up sponsors. Their parents helped while their aunt Gertrude worried about the race. "People get hurt in those things," she said.

Frank tried to calm her down. "Joe and I have been riding motorcycles for years," he said. "Our dad rode before us, and our grandparents before him. I remember reading an account of Hardys riding cycles as long ago as nineteen twenty-seven."

"Well, of course I wouldn't remember *that* far back," Gertrude said, flustered. With that, she took to the phone banks along with Fenton, Laura, and the two boys. Working together, the five of them scraped together a respectable number of contributions by the time of the party.

Unfortunately, the Hardys' girlfriends, Callie Shaw and Iola Morton, had already left for the long weekend. They had driven with Iola's brother, Chet, to the town of Jewel Ridge.

The brothers arrived at the VFW Memorial Hall, a relatively small, steel-sided building that used to house a nightclub, shortly after eight.

As they entered, they found the party already in full swing. Jamal waved at them when they came in. He was standing in a corner, chatting with Corri Fernandez. Her brother, Paco, hovered nearby, talking to Ed Henderson. Paco glanced protectively from Amber Hawk—surrounded by admirers near the refreshment table—to his younger sister.

Mr. Fernandez mingled with the crowd, shaking hands and smiling. Camera crew members from WBPT and other local TV stations followed him around like wolves circling their prey. To his credit, Mr. Fernandez refused to get annoyed with them.

Joe and Frank introduced themselves to Ed Henderson. They chatted with him for a few moments, then mingled with the rest of the crowd.

"Do you think we should say hello to Amber Hawk?" Joe asked.

"Let's wait until she talks to us," Frank said.

"That Corri Fernandez is one very brave girl,"

said a deep voice from behind the brothers. The Hardys turned as a tall man wearing an impeccable business suit stepped toward them. He stretched out one big hand to the brothers while still carrying a drink in the other. "I'm Asa Goldberg," he said as they shook hands, "one of the benefit's sponsors."

"Pleased to meet you," Frank said.

"What do you do, Mr. Goldberg?" Joe asked.

"I sell quality imports," Goldberg replied. "Many of Bayport's wealthiest citizens are my clients. I'm more than happy to lend my clout to a cause like this. In fact, I was the one who first proposed the races to Peter and his family."

"I'm sure the Fernandezes are grateful for your help," Joe said.

As the three of them spoke, Goldberg steered them toward a small stage near the back corner of the room. A podium sat atop the stage on the right. To the left, in front of a golden curtain, rested the grand prize—the restored O'Sullivan SD5 motorcycle.

Goldberg gazed at the silver and black cycle, and his brown eyes twinkled. "Isn't she a beaut?" he said.

"Sure is," Frank and Joe agreed. The machine looked to be in perfect condition, though neither of the brothers knew exactly what an SD5 was supposed to look like.

Several other people stood nearby, admiring the prize. One of them, a tall, slender man with a pinched face, said, "It's lovely, of course. But not nearly as valuable as it would be if more of its pieces were original."

"Now, don't cut down the grand prize, Trent," Goldberg said. He turned to the teens and said in a stage whisper, "That's Trent Howard—a notorious motorcycle collector. Don't let his complaints fool you. I bet he's wishing he could enter the race himself so he could win that set of wheels!"

"Why can't he?" Joe asked.

"No talent," Goldberg said a little louder, with a smile.

"Hey!" Trent Howard said, turning on him. "You talk pretty big for a man who's never even tried the circuit." Then, to Frank and Joe, he continued: "I made a go of it once, but I just had no aptitude. I'm a thinker, not a rider. And, in point of fact, I've made a lot of money thinking. That's how I can afford to collect motorcycles."

Howard was trying to play it cool, but the Hardys saw that Goldberg's cutting remark had actually needled him. The other people nearby watched the exchange curiously.

"So, are you sponsoring someone in the race?" Frank asked the collector.

"I'd rather not say," Howard replied.

"He certainly isn't sponsoring me," put in a nearby blonde. She was about the Hardys age and very slender, with her hair done up in double braids.

"I don't want you thinking I'm working with Mr. Howard just because I'm standing next to him."

"No one was accusing you of that, Ms. Navarro," Howard said.

A distinguished man with graying hair and a beard who was on the other side of the girl added, "Elizabeth is in this to win. Aren't you, dear?"

"Daaad!" she said, rolling her eyes. "Of course I want to win. You don't run a race to come in last! One day, you'll write about me the way you do about Garth Metzger."

"What made Metzger so special?" Joe asked.

"Let me explain," Trent Howard replied. "Garth Metzger was an old-time motorcycle rider and designer. On the verge of bankruptcy, he came up with an idea for a fabulous, new engine. He sketched those plans down, then made *one set* of blueprints from them."

"I know this part of the story," Goldberg continued. "Once Metzger completed his engine, he installed it in a cycle and then destroyed the blueprints. People who saw the engine tests said it was the best of its kind, ever. Buyers came from all over to bid on it."

"Dad wrote an article about that once, didn't you, Dad?" Elizabeth said. "Tell what happened next."

Richard Navarro seemed reluctant to speak up, so his daughter nudged him. "Well," he finally said, "Metzger thought he could get more money from the bidders if he won a race with the experimental bike. But something went wrong. He got into a fiery crash during the race and died. The super-engine was destroyed."

"It's ironic," Goldberg said. "He could have made a fortune, but instead, Metzger died penniless. They sold the contents of his garage. Later, some of those cycle parts got bought by Pops Fernandez, which is how they ended up in this bike here."

He pointed to the glittering SD5 displayed before them.

"So, are you advising your daughter, Richard?" Howard asked Navarro. "Or are you entering the race yourself?"

"My competing days are behind me," Rich Navarro said, shaking his head. "I don't have the stamina for it anymore. I'm sticking with motor-cycle magazine writing now. Maybe I could do a story on you, Mr. Howard."

Trent Howard frowned. "I've had all the public-ity I want, thank you very much."

"But it would make a great article," Navarro said. "Wealthy collector turns out for benefit motocross event—"

"Really, I'm only interested in the bike for histor-ical reasons," Howard insisted.

"If you want that bike, we could help you out," said a voice from the other side of the prize stand. The one who had spoken was a tall, blond man.

The woman with her arm around him was nearly as tall, and had short, straight, dark hair.

"Boy," Joe whispered to Frank, "you can't even finish a conversation here without someone cutting in."

"And who might you two be?" Trent Howard asked, arching one eyebrow at the newcomers.

The big man and the tall woman shook hands with Trent. "I'm Jules Kendallson," said the man. "And this is my girl, Sylvia Short."

The brothers noticed the irony of a tall woman being named "Short," but both managed to keep straight faces.

"We're freelance riders," Ms. Short declared.

"We like winning," Kendallson said, "but we ain't big collectors of cycles."

"More bikes, more repairs," Ms. Short added. "Y'know? We'd rather have the cash. How much you offering?"

Trent Howard cleared his throat. "While I'm somewhat fascinated with the Metzger SD5, I'm not interested in hiring freelance riders at this point."

"If you're keen on getting this bike, Mr. Howard, why didn't you just buy it from the Fernandezes?" Joe asked.

"I tried," Howard said, "but Mr. Fernandez wanted more than I was willing to pay. I may be well-off, but taking on the bulk of Corrine Fernandez's rehab bills . . . It's a hefty sum, and I just can't let all that cash go right now." He looked at Mr.

Goldberg and added, "I suspect the same is true of Asa, here."

"You got that right," Goldberg replied. "But I would if I could. As it is, I'm happy just to be making a contribution."

"As am I," Howard replied.

"Yeah, we're here for that, too," Kendallson said. Ms. Short and the Navarros nodded in support.

"Well, I'm sure Corri's glad to have all of you pulling for her," Frank said.

Goldberg, Howard, and the rest nodded again. Then, as if by silent agreement, they all moved away from the prize table.

"Let's grab something to eat," Joe said. "We were so busy rounding up pledges, we didn't stop for dinner."

The brothers made their way to the refreshment table and picked up some snacks and punch. Frank dropped a few dollars into a contribution jar at the end of the buffet.

"We don't want them to lose money putting on this party," he explained.

"It's a good turnout," Joe said. "I hope they do as well with the races. People seem to be having a good time too." He hooked a thumb to a corner where Corrine Fernandez and Jamal were chatting happily with some other racers.

Suddenly, a shriek ripped through the air: "Fire!"

33

4 Where There's Smoke . . .

Everyone was quiet until another voice shouted, "Fire!"

It was a different voice this time, and neither brother could place it. A billow of black smoke wafted across the ceiling of the room.

Chaos erupted in the small assembly hall. The crowd began to press for the exits.

"Everyone stay calm!" Frank called, but no one seemed to be listening.

Smoke came from behind some curtains near the prize stand and rapidly filled the room. Cries of panic went up as people bumped into one another in the gathering gloom.

"Jamal! Where are you?" Frank called. He waved

some of the smoke away from his face, but still couldn't see much.

"Here!" came Jamal's voice from near the side exit. He coughed as he shouted to the brothers. "Corri and I are stuck!"

"We're coming!" Joe said. He and Frank pushed their way through the crowd.

"Are you two all right?" Frank asked when they reached their friends.

"If you can help clear the crowd," Jamal said, "I can wheel Corri out of here."

"Sure thing," Joe said. He and Frank went to work. While being careful not to hurt anyone else, they moved quickly and forcefully toward the door. Jamal and Corri followed right behind. Several times, Frank and Joe paused to help people who had fallen. Soon the Hardys and their friends reached the doorway and went outside.

"Is everyone okay?" Frank asked.

Corrine Fernandez coughed hard but nodded that she was all right. Jamal nodded too. "Has anyone seen my brother?" Corri asked.

The Hardys and Jamal shook their heads.

"Maybe he's around front," Jamal suggested.

"You go check," Frank said. "Joe and I will help other people out."

The brothers stood near the door, calling to people

to help them find their way through the gloom. Fortunately, most folks seemed to have gotten out of the smoky building on their own. The Hardys ventured inside a couple of times, holding their breath while they helped a victim through the thick black smoke.

After a few minutes, Jamal dashed back around from the other side of the building. With him came Elizabeth Navarro, who looked very worried.

"Paco and Pops got out okay," Jamal reported. "In fact, everyone scheduled to attend the event is accounted for—"

"Except my dad," Elizabeth reported. "No one knows where he is."

Joe, who was standing next to the door, called out, "Mr. Navarro! Are you in there! Make a sound if you need help!"

"Dad! Dad! Can you hear me?" Elizabeth shouted.

She and the Hardys listened intently, but all they heard was the murmur of the crowd and the sound of distant fire engine sirens.

"Those rescue workers won't get here soon enough to help Navarro if he's trapped," Frank said.

Joe nodded his agreement. "It looks like we'll have to go in."

"I'll go with you," Jamal offered.

"No," Joe said. "No sense three of us risking our lives. You stay here and keep the rest of the party-goers back." He glanced meaningfully at Elizabeth

Navarro, who looked as though she might run inside at any moment.

"Yeah, okay," Jamal said.

"Don't worry, Ms. Navarro," Frank said. "We'll get your dad out safely."

With that, he and his brother plunged back into the smoky building. The Hardys pulled their T-shirts up over their noses in a kind of makeshift smoke filter, but it didn't do much good. Within moments, their eyes were burning and their lungs were stinging.

Frank coughed and called, "Mr. Navarro!"

Before he and Joe had taken five steps, someone stumbled out of the darkness, almost bowling them over. "I'm Navarro," the man said, coughing. "Which way is the exit?"

Joe and Frank hurried him back outside.

"Dad!" Elizabeth said, throwing her arms around her father. "I was so worried!"

"I'm okay," Navarro replied. "I just got turned around in the darkness."

Moments later, the fire and rescue squad roared up outside the old VFW building. The firefighters moved to quickly control the problem, while the EMTs checked over those who had inhaled too much smoke or had been injured in the stampede. Though Richard Navarro seemed reluctant to receive any attention, Elizabeth dragged her father to see the medics.

The brothers, Jamal, and Corri made their way around to the front of the building to join the rest of the former partygoers. It was a big, restless crowd. Local TV cameras, and other media reporters, pushed through the throng, taping reactions to the incident.

The fire department quickly brought the smoke under control. Apparently, the blaze hadn't been as bad as it had looked. Some old rags in a broom closet near the back hallway had caught fire, and other things stored in the closet had fueled the smoke.

"It was a lot more smoke than fire," Chief Hebert reported to the partygoers. "Still, I'm glad you all got out safely."

The police showed up and took statements. Many people complained that they'd lost wallets and other valuables.

"That's not unusual in this kind of confusion," Con Riley, one of the attending officers, said. "Chances are, the missing pieces will turn up once the room is cleaned and straightened out." Still, he dutifully wrote down every lost item in his notebook.

Pops Fernandez looked worried. He'd been talking almost nonstop to the TV and other media crews since the rescue workers had arrived. "This is terrible," he whispered to his children, who were resting curbside near the Hardys and Jamal.

"At least no one was hurt," Corri said.

"She's right," Paco replied. "And the publicity from the fire may even help promote the race."

Mr. Fernandez glared at his son. "What a terrible thing to say. The media are going to eat us alive."

"The fire wasn't your fault," Joe interjected. "The newspeople are bound to see that."

"Maybe," Mr. Fernandez agreed. He looked apprehensively back at the now-empty building. "Fortunately, it looks like the SD5 wasn't damaged. That's the last thing we need on top of everything else."

Sensing that the Fernandezes wanted to be alone, the Hardys and Jamal headed back to their cars.

The brothers said good-bye to Jamal in the parking lot, then returned to their house. Their parents and Aunt Gertrude were already asleep.

As they headed up to bed, Frank whispered to Joe, "What a day. Corrine nearly got killed by a runaway cycle. Then there was the office burglary. And finally, the fire at the party." He paused for a minute. "Think it may be more than coincidence?"

Joe nodded. "Yeah. Let's not forget the wallets and other things that went missing during the confusion. A fire is a pretty handy distraction for a pickpocket."

"Right," said Frank. "Good thing the SD5 was too big to smuggle out of the club under someone's coat."

"We'll really have to keep our eyes peeled during

this race," Joe commented. "Otherwise, Corri may never get that rehab she needs."

Early the next morning, the brothers headed out to the Fernandez dirt track. They'd been assigned a "garage" space—which was more like a medium-sized storage locker in a big, metal building near the race track. Once there, they took some time to tune up their bikes.

"We should take these out more often," Joe said. "I really like riding. Remember that time we rode down Bay Road to that house by the cliffs?"

"That was an adventure," Frank agreed. "Seems like ages ago."

"I know," Joe said. "Sometimes I feel like we've been solving mysteries for the better part of a century. Let's hope we don't have to do much detecting during the races, though. We'll need to concentrate to have any chance of winning."

"We're lucky that contestants are limited to 125 cc engines," Frank said. "Otherwise, the more experienced racers would completely outclass us." He finished tightening a spark plug.

The roar of a motorcycle engine caught their attention as Jamal rode up. "I don't know whether you guys are early birds or late risers," he said.

"How come?" Joe asked.

"Well, you got here before I did," Jamal said, "so you're early. On the other hand, you're still working on your bikes, and the events are nearly ready to start."

"You tuned up your bike at home?" Frank deduced.

"Yep," Jamal said. "She's purring like a kitten."

"Home tune-ups were out for us," Joe said.

"Unless we wanted Aunt Gertrude hovering around while we worked," Frank added. "And we definitely didn't. She's worried about us competing."

"I hear you," Jamal said. "I'm glad my dad is so cool about this kind of thing."

"Well, he runs an air taxi service," Joe said, "which isn't the safest profession in the world."

"We've had a few scrapes over the years," Jamal admitted, "but we've always come out on top." He got off his bike and helped the brothers make a few final adjustments. "They told you I was sharing your garage, right?" he asked. "Three to a 'cubbyhole' in this place."

"There are a lot more racers than they usually have, I guess," Frank said.

"Well, at least we all know one another," Jamal said. "Some of the other racers are working elbow to elbow with people they either don't know or don't like."

"Who are Amber Hawk and Ed Henderson sharing with?" Frank asked.

"Are you kidding?" Jamal replied. "The big names don't have to share with anyone."

"One of the perks of being a big name," Joe noted.

"I bet their sponsors are paying for that privilege, though," Frank said.

"Let's hope," Jamal said. "The Fernandezes can use all the dough they can get. Especially after last night. The VFW is griping about their insurance company not wanting to pay for the fire damage."

"Well, that stinks," Joe said. "What are insurance companies for if they don't pay for accidents?"

"Was it an accident, though?" Frank asked rhetorically.

"Leave that to the police and concentrate on your riding," Jamal said. "I saw Ed Henderson working out earlier. He'll be tough to beat. Acrobatics are his specialty."

"I just hope to stay on my bike!" Joe said.

"We haven't had much time to practice," Frank admitted. "And we don't have a change of seats, like I've heard some riders do."

"It's true. A custom seat can make doing aerobatic stunts much easier," Jamal said.

"Come on," Frank said, wiping down his bike one last time. "Let's get out to the track. The opening ceremonies are starting pretty soon."

As Corri had told them, the whoopdedoos had been turned into larger hills for the day's event. The earthworks weren't as tall as they would have been for a contest of pure acrobatics, but they were much taller than the bumps on the usual dirt motocross track. The whole speedway looked as though it were covered with monstrous anthills.

On their way to the course, the boys ran into Mr. Fernandez chatting with the contestants before the race. "Good luck today," he said to Marissa Hayday as he headed toward the Hardys and Jamal.

"Thanks," Marissa replied. "Good luck to you, too. I hope you make a lot of money." She turned and walked over to two girls whom the Hardys figured must be her sisters.

"I'm glad she decided to ride," Jamal said.

"Me too," Mr. Fernandez said, smiling. "Let's hope last night's incident is the last of our troubles."

"Do the police have any ideas about what caused the fire?" Frank asked.

"They can't be sure yet, but they're thinking someone might have deliberately set it," Pops replied. "Most of the wallets and watches that went missing never turned up."

"So they're thinking this was some kind of robbery," Joe said.

"I hope the media play it that way," Pops said, "rather than as trouble with the benefit. If we're lucky, today's race will turn the publicity bandwagon around. No one's ever done a competition like this before. And the acrobatic-aerobatic Mixed Freestyle is absolutely unique in the history of motocross. Now, if you'll excuse me, I have to get up to the announcing stand. See you at the start of the race."

The Hardys and Jamal joined the other contestants gathering near the grandstand. The armored riders and polished cycles almost made the racers look like knights at a medieval tournament.

"Do people seem nervous to you?" Joe asked. He looked from the old hands, like Henderson and Hawk, to the up-comers like Hayday, Navarro, Kendallson, Short, and dozens of others. All were milling around apprehensively, except for Hawk and Henderson, who spent part of their time eyeing each other and the rest of their time signing autographs for fans and other racers.

"Well, I'll be . . . ," Jamal began.

"What's wrong?" Frank asked.

"See that dim-looking guy over there?" Jamal asked. He pointed to a buff teen with a shaved head. "That's Justin Davies."

"Didn't he beat you out at last year's midtown baseball tryouts?" Joe asked.

"That's the guy," Jamal replied. "He's always looking to one-up me. He must have heard I was racing and decided to get in on the action. He'll do anything to get my goat. He nearly ran me over at a crosswalk last week. Then he tried to make it look like it was my fault."

"Let's try to keep out of his way, then," Frank

said. "We've got enough to worry about in this race without old school rivalries flaring up."

Davies spotted them, though. He revved his engine and raced his bike around the intervening crowd, then skidded it to a stop right next to Jamal. He hit a nearby puddle with his back tire, splattering Jamal's clean racing outfit with mud. "Hey, sorry, Hawkins," Davies said. "I didn't see you there."

"That is *it*, Davies!" Jamal said. He threw off his riding gloves and charged the bully.

5 Down & Dirty

Jamal jumped toward Davies before the Hardys could intervene. The shaved-headed teen got off his bike and tackled Jamal first. Both riders crashed onto the soggy earth.

The two of them rolled around on the ground like football players fighting for a fumble. Joe tried to pull Jamal up but got kicked on the chin for his trouble.

Frank caught his younger brother as Joe fell back.

"Looks like I owe Davies one as well," Joe said angrily.

"Take it easy," Frank cautioned. "We don't want to make things worse." He tried to step in too, but the rolling, flailing bodies kept him at a distance.

A crowd gathered around the brawling contestants. A few security guards standing by noticed the fight too. They made a beeline for Jamal and Davies.

The two racers broke apart and rolled to their feet. Jamal stared at his rival, anger burning in his brown eyes. Davies smiled, ready to jump Jamal again. The crowd pressed in around the fighters, separating them from Frank and Joe, who were still looking to stop the fight.

Suddenly, they heard the roar of a powerful motorcycle engine. All eyes turned as Ed Henderson's blue custom bike soared through the air, right toward the group.

The gawkers dove for cover. Jamal and Davies ducked out of the way as Henderson landed between them. The stunt rider spun his bike in a circle, kicking up the dirt with his rear wheel. Jamal, the Hardys, and the rest backed away.

"Well, that's one way to break up a fight," Joe said to Frank.

"Risky, but effective," Frank agreed.

Henderson skidded his motorcycle to a halt and took off his helmet. His long brown hair fell to his shoulders, and his intense blue eyes peered at each of the combatants. "Are you two here to race or to fight?" he said angrily.

"Who asked you to butt in?" Davies said.

Joe and Frank made their way to Jamal's side. "Take it easy, Jamal," Frank whispered. "You don't want to get kicked out of this race."

"I guess you're right," Jamal said through clenched teeth. "Getting thrown out wouldn't do Corri any good."

As the shock of the impromptu stunt wore off, the crowd that had gathered around Henderson applauded. TV cameras converged rapidly on the spot, surrounding him. The stunt rider smiled.

Davies glared at him, then picked up his bike out of the dirt and trotted away before security could catch up with him. Jamal righted his motorcycle as well. "Guess I'd better face the music," he said. He took a deep breath, then walked over to meet the guards.

"I hope they don't disqualify him," Frank said to Joe.

"I doubt they will," Joe replied. "Remember, they need every pledge rider that they can get."

Henderson's fight-ending stunt had shifted the media's attention from the brawlers to him. The pro rider looked happy to play to the crowd and grant interviews.

Amber Hawk, standing near the Hardys, didn't seem very pleased with Henderson's grandstanding. She gritted her teeth and muttered, "Hotdog!" then returned to fiddling with her motorcycle.

After speaking to the guards for few minutes, Jamal rejoined the brothers. "They just gave me a stern warning," he said. "I got lucky."

Finally, the crowd settled down, and everyone

seemed ready to start the day's competition.

Pops Fernandez and his family ascended to the announcing platform across from the grandstand. Paco, dressed in a racing outfit and armor, pushed Corri up a specially built ramp so she could take her place at the microphones alongside her father.

Peter Fernandez stepped up to the mike and cleared his throat. "Welcome," he said, his voice booming over the track's PA system, "to the Corrine Fernandez Benefit Challenge—a unique motocross event!"

The crowd roared their approval as the racers assembled next to the track.

Mr. Fernandez continued. "I want to thank our friends at UAN—the United America Network— for making this fund-raiser a nationwide broadcast!"

Again, the crowd exploded into applause and cheers.

"I'd also like to thank our friends in the local media, especially WBPT and the Bayport *Journal-Times* for their ongoing support," Mr. Fernandez said.

"Also, I'd like to thank our sponsors," Mr. Fernandez said, and indicated a group of distinguished-looking guests sitting to one side of the reviewing stand. Asa Goldberg, Trent Howard, and the other people assembled there smiled and nodded. "And a special thank-you to the professional motocross racers, Amber Hawk and Ed

Henderson, who generously agreed to participate in this series without their usual appearance fees.

"This racing benefit would not be possible without the tireless efforts on the part of many, many people. Foremost among them are the racers themselves, and the many sponsors who have pledged to support them. It is to all of you that we really owe our greatest gratitude," Mr. Fernandez finished.

The crowd roared especially loudly at this, and the racers down near the track stomped their feet and banged on their racing armor, making a real racket. Joe, Frank, and Jamal joined in.

"Now," Pops said, "I'd like to turn the microphone over to my daughter, Corrine, whom you are all so generously supporting. Corri will explain the rules of this unique race series."

As Corri rolled up to the mike, the crowd went wild, cheering, whistling, and shouting her name.

Corri smiled and waved at them. "Thanks, Pops," she said. "And thank you, all of you, for participating in this race. When I was injured last year, I thought the world had ended. Now, thanks to your kindness and support, I'm feeling better about things—like it's not the end."

The crowd applauded. A few people shouted, "We love you, Corri!" Frank noticed several nearby racers wiping tears from the corners of their eyes.

Corri took a deep breath. "And I *will* get out of

this wheelchair. With your help, I will not only walk again, I will *ride* again!"

All the people assembled went wild with applause and cheering. A chant of "Corri! Corri!" built up within the ranks of the racers.

Now it was Corri's turn to wipe a tear from her cheek. She composed herself, then began speaking again. "Thank you," she said. "Now, I didn't just come up here to give a pep talk. I came to explain the rules of this series of challenge races.

"As most of you know, there are three phases to this unique motocross event—the acrobatic/aerobatic mixed race, the traditional dirt track race, and the Enduro, a cross-country race. Racers will be using the same 125 cc motorcycles during each day of the event. Riders may make adjustments to suspension, tires, seats, and engine performance between each event—but the bike must remain the same. The use of standard-engine cycles will make the benefit exciting for all racers, from novice to experienced. During the first two phases of the competition, points will be awarded to each rider, depending on how she or he finishes in the races.

"Those points will be used to determine the starting order of riders in the final phase of the race, as well as the time differential between riders. If you build up a lot of points today and tomorrow, you will have a good head start during the final day of the competition. Whoever crosses the finish line first on

Sunday is the winner." She smiled at the pack of assembled racers. They cheered enthusiastically.

Joe noticed Amber Hawk and Ed Henderson eyeing each other. "Clearly those two think they're going to be in the top spots on Sunday," he whispered to Frank.

"So that's the overall picture," Corri continued. "You can find the exact details in the information packets you received when registering for the race, in the program booklets on sale at the concession stands, or online at the Fernandez Cycle Track Web site.

"Now that we've got those preliminaries over with, I can explain the rules for today's race." She took a deep breath. "This is not your usual motocross event. Today's Mixed Freestyle race combines elements of traditional motocross racing with elements of motorcycling acrobatics. Heats in the event will be timed, but points will also be awarded for acrobatic stunts performed during the race. The more difficult the stunts, the more points awarded."

She pointed to the motocross track, with its unusually high whoopdedoos. The Hardys and Jamal took measure of the course. Elizabeth Navarro, standing nearby, fiddled nervously with the strap of her blue motorcycle helmet. Frank noticed that the helmet had a white skull painted on the side.

"The point system makes it possible," Corri said, "to win today's event without actually crossing the finish line first. Of course, the best racers will combine both speed and acrobatics."

Ed Henderson and Amber Hawk smiled confidently.

"Because of the dangerous nature of this event," Corrine continued, "the number of racers in each heat will be smaller than usual. Each rider will compete only once. The racer with the highest total of points will be the leader going into tomorrow's event. Any questions?"

No one had any.

"All right," Corri said. "Get your bikes ready—because it's time to ride!"

The racers gave a huge cheer, and the crowd in the stands applauded. The cyclists started their engines and showed off a little for the spectators.

Meanwhile, Marissa Hayday chatted animatedly with her sisters, Elena and Karina, who were serving as her pit crew for the competition. Richard Navarro was talking to his daughter.

"Remember," Frank and Joe overheard the magazine writer say, "you don't have to win this phase of the race. Just give it a good run, and stay safe." Elizabeth nodded and pulled on her helmet.

"That skull on her helmet doesn't seem like a very good symbol for her," Joe remarked. "She seems skittish as a newborn kitten."

"I talked to her at the party last night," Jamal said. "The emblem used to be her dad's in his cycle club days. She's wearing it for good luck."

"Let's hope she doesn't need it," Joe said.

"At least a couple of people don't seem to have the prerace jitters," Frank noted. He hooked a thumb to where Ed Henderson and Amber Hawk were standing in the middle of a huge crowd, still signing autographs for fans.

"Hawk doesn't usually sign autographs much," Jamal said. "I guess she's just trying to compete with Henderson."

"Whoever wins this event will be king of the hill for a while, that's for sure," Joe said.

"The trouble with being king of the hill," Frank noted, "is that someone is always trying to push you off the top."

The brothers and their friend headed for the pits to make final preparations for the race. All three of them knew that this phase of the race would be particularly tricky and dangerous, so they wanted to make sure they were ready.

Being last-minute entrants, the brothers hadn't been able to line anyone up for their pit crew. But Jamal pitched in, and in return, the Hardys helped him with his bike.

After tuning up, the three friends took turns securing one another's racing armor.

Through luck of the draw, Joe came up in one of

the earliest heats. He would be competing against Ed Henderson, Amber Hawk, Sylvia Short, and a racer named Taylor Fohr.

"I doubt I'll be the top finisher in this one," Joe said ruefully.

"Don't give up," Frank replied. "Maybe you'll pull an upset."

"Or you could let Hawk and Henderson take the limelight and just put in your fastest speed," Jamal suggested. "With them concentrating on each other, you may be able to slip in under the radar."

Frank and Jamal got Joe into his starting position on the course. Then Frank found a good spot to watch his brother, and Jamal went back to preparing for his heat.

The day had grown warm and sticky. The smell of dirt and motorcycle exhaust hung in the air. Corrine Fernandez was going to be doing the play-by-play, announcing from her perch on the tower overlooking the track. Her pleasant voice boomed through the loudspeakers above the grandstand: "And . . . they're off!"

Almost immediately Hawk and Henderson zoomed out to a big lead. The two of them raced neck and neck as they hit the first jump. Joe, Fohr, and Short trailed behind.

Henderson got huge air on the first tall whoopdedoo, catapulting his bike into the sky. He executed a "Superman" flyoff, hanging his whole body in the air over the saddle, then landed solidly on the downslope. Hawk had gotten ahead of him, but the stunt she performed hadn't been nearly so spectacular.

"A *monstrous* trick by Henderson!" Corri's voice said.

Joe gunned the throttle and zipped over the hill, catching a bit of air as he did so. He didn't try anything fancy, wanting to get a feel for the course first. His steady progress put him in third place, behind the two leaders. He spotted Frank, watching from beyond the next rise, then lost sight of him as he hit the ground again.

Hawk topped the next hill before Henderson. She did a barhop over her handlebars as she went, then disappeared behind the hill.

Henderson topped the next rise, gunning his throttle all the way as he went up. He hit the top of the whoopdedoo in a nearly vertical climb and twisted his bike into the first somersault in a combination.

Man and machine hung gracefully in the air for a moment—then Henderson's black and gold motorcycle exploded.

6 Flameout

A ball of orange fire burst around the cycle as it flew to pieces. Henderson soared head over heels into the air right in front of Joe's onrushing bike.

Joe ducked as a flaming gas tank flew by, barely missing the top of his helmet. He swerved to avoid a bouncing tire. Several small pieces of burning shrapnel bounced off the younger Hardy's riding armor.

Henderson's limp body flashed by as Joe crested the hill. He braked into a jump, not caring about amplitude or difficulty, just fighting to maintain control.

At the bottom of the hill, Frank stood wide-eyed with shock.

"Look out!" he yelled.

Somehow, Joe heard him above the roar of the engine and the bang of the explosion.

Joe ducked again, and one of Henderson's shock absorbers glanced off his helmet.

The younger Hardy swerved and almost went into a skid. He put his left foot down, and felt a lance of pain shoot up his leg. But his boot steadied the bike, and he kept on going.

Frank ran forward, glancing at Joe to make sure his brother was all right. When Joe kept riding, the elder Hardy sprinted to the scene of the crash. Seeing his brother running to help Henderson, Joe decided to stay in the race.

The roar of motorcycle engines and the whine of sirens filled the air. Frank ignored them and angled for Henderson's body, lying prone amid the flaming wreckage of his black and gold cycle.

Sylvia Short topped the rise and headed directly toward the crash, with Taylor Fohr right beside her. Both riders swerved and nearly went down. They kicked great clouds of dirt into the air; Frank shielded his eyes to keep from being blinded.

As Frank reached the injured cyclist, Joe crested the next berm and disappeared from view, with Fohr and Short hot on his tail.

Frank used his first aid skills to stabilize Henderson until the real paramedics showed up. Some of the cyclist's limbs looked broken, and he probably had a concussion. Henderson's riding armor had protected him from some of the damage, but cycle fuel had splashed onto it, setting it aflame in a few places. Frank smothered the small fires, then did what he could until the ambulances arrived.

Race officials red-flagged the race, meaning the other contestants had to stop until the course was cleared. Frank helped the paramedics load Henderson into the ambulance. He watched with some annoyance as news crews followed the injured man out of the stadium.

"They're like vultures," he heard someone beside him say.

It was Marissa Hayday. She and her two sisters, Elena and Karina, had come to try to help. "Why can't they just leave people alone?" Karina, the middle sister, said.

"They're just doing their job," Elena noted. "Speaking of which, we've got to get Marissa ready for her race."

Marissa nodded grimly. "The show must go on," she said.

Frank went back to his bike as well.

The race resumed just as soon as the ambulance left. Joe crossed the finish line second, but placed third when acrobatics were taken into account. Amber Hawk finished first. Taylor Fohr edged out Joe on points. He seemed surprised at his placement and grinned all the way off the course.

"Are you all right, Joe?" Frank asked as he walked up to his brother.

"Jarred my leg a bit," the younger Hardy said, "but other than that, I'm fine. How's Henderson?"

"He looked pretty bad," Frank admitted. "We were lucky none of the other racers hit us while I was trying to help him."

"He'll pull through," Joe said. "He's been through some tough scrapes before."

"His being out of the race sure puts Amber Hawk in a good position," Frank commented.

"Yeah," Joe agreed. "He was her main competition in this event. Even with the strange series format, I doubt anyone else will be able to beat her."

Frank rubbed his chin.

Joe understood the gesture. "You're thinking that Hawk might have had something to do with Henderson's crash?"

"It's possible," Frank said. "Someone could have sabotaged his bike while he was signing autographs."

"But she was right there, signing with him," Joe said.

"Not the whole time," Frank noted. "And she could have had an accomplice."

"Or it could just have been an accident."

"A midair explosion like that, on a bike driven by one of the top motocross racers in the country?" Frank said. "It doesn't seem likely."

"Maybe the police report can clue us in," Joe said. "Your race is coming up—are you ready?"

"As ready as I'll ever be," Frank said, pulling on his riding gloves and helmet.

"Try my tactic," Joe said. "Go fast and make the jumps as big as you can handle. We're not acrobats, so just try to be fast."

Frank drew the same heat as Paco Fernandez, who was competing to honor his sister. The elder Hardy fought hard during the race. He hit some soaring jumps and ultimately clocked a good time. It wasn't enough to beat Paco, though, who even finished ahead of Hawk in the standings.

Corrine's brother seemed quite pleased with his placing. "Guess I showed that you don't have to be famous to turn in a good ride," he said to reporters afterward.

Jamal did even better in his heat than Frank. He pulled off a couple of cool acrobatic moves during his run, including a no-footed can-can and a cowboy split. He posted a good time, too, and both brothers rushed to meet their friend after his run.

"Great ride, Jamal!" Joe enthused.

"Excellent!" Frank agreed.

Jamal pulled off his helmet and wiped the sweat from his forehead. "I almost skidded coming out of that cowboy," he said. "I was lucky."

"That was more a sign of practice than luck, I

think," Frank said. "Now that all of us are finished with the Mixed Freestyle, we can relax a bit while they run the rest of the heats."

"Sounds like a plan," Jamal said. "Who's in the last run?"

Joe checked the printed schedule they'd been given that morning. "Jules Kendallson, Marissa Hayday, Elizabeth Navarro, and two people I've never heard of," he said.

Jamal glanced over his shoulder at the paper. "Marissa should have a good chance in that group—assuming her sisters have stopped bickering long enough to prep her bike properly."

"They seem like a pretty feisty trio," Joe said. "What's the deal with them?"

"They've done everything as a team practically since they were born," Jamal replied. "Elena and Karina ride motocross too, and they're pretty good. But I think they decided to maximize their winning potential by backing Marissa, who has the most experience."

"It's good having family to help you out in the pits," Frank said.

"Yeah," Jamal agreed. "Though it has its drawbacks, especially if a squabble breaks out."

"Hey, want to grab some food?" Joe asked. "We can check the final standings afterward."

"I'd love to, but I promised Corrine I'd catch up

with her after my heat," Jamal said. "We'll compare notes for tomorrow's dirt-track run later, though. Okay?"

"Sounds like a plan," Frank said. "We'll catch up with you at our garage bay after they shoo out the public."

"Great," Jamal said. "See you then." He took his bike back to the makeshift garage, then headed up to the announcing tower to see Corri, who was still covering the race.

The brothers, who had already put their cycles away, headed for the concession stand. They got a good view of the track on the way, and caught a bit of the action. Marissa Hayday seemed to be driving well. Her pink and purple bike whipped around the track, getting good air on the whoopdedoos. Jules Kendallson rode fairly well, but almost wiped out after a big jump. His bike hit the ground hard, and his armored shins brushed against the dirt as he turned.

"Ouch!" Joe said. "I bet he's glad to have on that black and green armor. Otherwise he'd be picking rocks out of his legs for weeks."

"Elizabeth Navarro's not doing much better," Frank said. "Look, she's gone down again."

As they watched, the young rider hit the bottom of a berm and spilled off her bike. Her yellow and black riding armor protected her, though.

She scrambled to her feet and got back in the race.

"And the skull on her helmet keeps on grinning!" Joe said.

Frank chuckled. "You have to admire her determination—and her dad's enthusiasm." He looked to the pits near the track, where Richard Navarro was jumping up and down, rooting for his girl.

The brothers grabbed some bratwurst and sodas from the concession stand, then decided to take a walk around the grounds as they ate. The track lay on the west side of the fenced-in area, with an extension of the course running off to the north. Thick woods abutted that side of the property. The brothers spotted several trails running from the edges of the dirt track into the trees.

"That must be part of the cross-country course for Sunday's Enduro race," Frank deduced.

"Right," Joe said, confirming the information on the map that had come in their registration packet.

From there, they looped back past the edge of the metal-walled garages and prep areas. They checked the office, which seemed both deserted and secure, then circled toward the main gate on the south. As they walked, they had a good view of the industrial property to the east, which seemed to manufacture enormous concrete pipes.

"This is a pretty nice course," Frank said, gazing around the Fernandez compound. "Too bad they've been struggling financially. I wonder how they're doing at the box office?"

"It looks like they're closing it down right now," Joe said, gazing at the small kiosk near the front gate.

As the last race wound to its conclusion, spectators drifted from the stands and toward their cars in the nearby parking lot. Some cars were already rumbling down the dirt driveway past the gate.

A short, dark-haired woman came out of the brightly painted kiosk near the raceway's main entrance. In her hands she held a big, gray cashbox. A tall man in black riding leathers and wearing a scuffed-up black helmet came out of the building a few steps behind her. The two of them headed toward Pops Fernandez's office, on the east side of the property.

"The size of the crowd should indicate a good take today," Frank said.

"Tomorrow's crowd will probably be better," Joe said. "It'll be Saturday, for one thing. And I'm sure the publicity from the Henderson crash will bring more people through the door."

Frank shook his head. "I hate to think of people—even nice folks like the Fernandezes—profiting from a serious accident."

Joe nodded his agreement. "It would be ironic if Henderson's injuries helped pay for Corri's rehab." He cast his eyes back to the woman leaving the box office. "You think that guy with her is security?" Joe asked. "That's an odd outfit for a guard."

"Maybe it's part of the show," Frank said, "to make the guards look like race participants or something."

The woman and man walked across a deserted space between the front gate and the office. Frank and Joe were the only people with a clear look at the pair. Buildings blocked everyone else's view of people leaving the track.

It was a good thing the Hardys could see— because suddenly, without warning, the helmeted man pulled a blackjack from his pocket and hit the woman carrying the cashbox over the back of the head.

7 Thousands to One

The weighted leather sack came down heavily on the woman's skull. She grunted and fell to the ground. The heavy gray cashbox spilled from her arms and landed in the dirt.

The helmeted man stooped down to pick it up.

"Hey, you! Stop!" Frank shouted. He and Joe, still several hundred yards away from the scene, dashed toward the leather-dressed assailant.

The man noticed the brothers, but focused his efforts on the box. He tried to pry the lid open with his black-gloved hands, but it wouldn't give. As the Hardys sprinted closer, he put away his blackjack and fished a knife out of his pocket.

The bandit jabbed at the cashbox lock with the point of the blade. It did no good. As the brothers closed in on him, he hefted the box, turned, and ran.

"I'll get him," Frank said as Joe skidded to a halt beside the injured woman.

The younger Hardy knelt at the woman's side as his brother continued running. "She's knocked out," Joe shouted to Frank. "I'll stay here and get her some medical attention."

The older Hardy didn't bother to reply. He knew Joe would do everything he could for the woman.

Frank and the thief ran across the unmowed lawn between the office area and the back row of metal garages. The culprit seemed about as tall as Frank, and nearly as fast. But the awkward weight of the big, metal cashbox slowed him down.

Frank smiled slightly.

Suddenly, the thief turned and threw the cashbox at the elder Hardy.

A gasp of air escaped Frank's lips as the big, metal container hit him in the gut. The box, still not open, landed on the ground between Frank and the bandit. Frank fell to his knees, clutching his stomach. The thief kept running.

Frank got up. He didn't dare leave the cashbox behind, though he knew carrying it would slow him down. He hefted the metal container and took off after the culprit once more.

The helmeted man ducked between two garages and into the pits beside the track. Mechanics and racers tending to their bikes filled the pit areas. No one even looked up as the helmeted man dashed through the crowd.

"Stop that guy!" Frank yelled as he entered the pits.

By then, though, the bandit had passed through the row of competitors and onto the track's main concourse. The race featuring Jules Kendallson, Elizabeth Navarro, and Marissa Hayday had just finished. A throng of spectators heading for their cars crowded the thoroughfare.

Corrine Fernandez's happy voice boomed over the loudspeaker: "Thanks for coming to the benefit today! We at the Fernandez Cycle Track hope you'll join us again tomorrow, for the *motocross* phase of this exciting challenge series!"

Frank shouted again for help, but no one heard him over the noise of the PA system.

The audience milling about blocked Frank from catching his quarry—and the big, heavy cashbox made navigation through them impossible. Frank spotted the culprit one last time near the far edge of the concourse, then lost sight of him in the crowd. By the time the elder Hardy pushed through the mob, the would-be robber had disappeared.

Frustrated, Frank headed back to where he'd left Joe. He found both an ambulance and Pops Fernandez waiting when he got back. Joe spotted

Frank as the EMTs loaded the injured woman into the ambulance.

"Are you okay?" Joe called to his brother. "Did you catch him?"

Frank shook his head. "He threw the cashbox at me and got away. I might have nabbed him, but I didn't want to leave the box behind." He handed the big, metal container to Pops Fernandez.

"Thank you," Pops said. "I don't know what we would have done if that bandit had gotten away with the day's receipts."

"How's the girl?" Frank asked.

"She'll be all right," Joe said. "The EMTs said she was only stunned. They're taking her to the hospital for observation—just in case."

"You two probably saved her life," Pops said.

"I think the robber was only interested in the money," Frank said. "I'm sorry I didn't catch him."

"Next time, you should post a real guard with your gate employee," Joe told Mr. Fernandez.

"We did," Pops replied. "But he'd taken a coffee break. When someone knocked on the box office door, Candy—the girl who got hit—told me she'd assumed it was the guard returning. She said the thief pushed his way in, then forced her to walk away from the main entrance. We could have lost thousands of dollars, all because of one moment of carelessness."

As the ambulance pulled away, the news media

caught wind that something was going on. They converged like vultures toward the spot where the brothers and Pops were standing.

Peter Fernandez sighed. "I'll take care of them," he said. "You boys get some rest. You deserve it."

"Have you called the police?" Frank asked.

"One of the cops stationed at the track called the main station," Pops replied.

"I already talked to that officer," Joe said. "So we don't have to stick around, unless you found out who the bandit was."

Frank shook his head. "No such luck."

Pops shook both their hands. "Again, thanks. It could have been a real disaster," he said.

"No problem," Joe replied.

He and Frank headed back to their garage unit to make some final preparations on their bikes and lock up for the night.

"So," Joe said as they walked, "do you think today's thief was the same guy who broke into the office last night?"

"Maybe," Frank replied. "With both wearing cycling outfits, there's no way to tell for sure."

"The helmet implies he might be a racer," Joe said.

Frank shrugged. "Or it could just have been a convenient disguise. At a place like this, a helmeted man wouldn't stick out much—unlike a man with a ski mask over his head."

"I'm sure we'll catch this guy in the end, whoever he is," Joe said.

His older brother nodded thoughtfully. "Participating in the race might make a good cover if you actually wanted to steal either the cashbox or one of the prizes," he said.

"You think someone might have entered the competition just to rob it?"

"It's possible," Frank said. "It could be someone without a lot of riding talent—like Elizabeth Navarro, for instance—just looking to make a big score. Competing would be a perfect cover."

"Very perfect in Navarro's case," Joe said. "She was actually on the track when the robbery took place."

"Yeah," Frank said. "That rules her out, along with the other racers who were on the course at the time."

"That only leaves about fifty suspects—not counting the spectators," Joe noted wryly.

Frank sighed. "It's a place to start, anyway."

"We can think about it tonight," Joe said. "Let's check the standings and hook up with Jamal, then head for home."

"Sounds good to me," Frank said. He rubbed his gut where the box had hit it. "I'm beat."

They found Jamal at the garage bay and filled him in on what had happened. Then they all locked up and checked the standings before they left.

"The rankings are close," Joe said, looking over the sheet. "Paco's got a lead, but not a commanding one."

"Hawk will have an advantage tomorrow," Jamal noted. "Motocross is her specialty."

"She got a lucky break when Henderson crashed," Frank said. "He was her main competition, but anyone could still take the series."

"The next two days will tell," Joe said.

The brothers arrived at the race course early the next morning to prepare their bikes for the day. Since the day's theme was standard motocross, as opposed to acrobatics, they changed the stiffness on their shock absorbers and put on tires with more aggressive treads. Many of other the racers changed their seats as well; specially cut saddles, making dismount tricks easier, were standard for pros competing in acrobatic cycle contests.

The top finishers in each race would ride against one another in the semifinals, then the finals. Placement in the last race of the day would determine the standings and start times for Sunday's Enduro.

Joe and Frank worked side by side with Jamal in their small assigned garage. Their space was connected to the adjoining bays by a long corridor running across the back. Small doors kept each garage separate from the common hallway. Big garage doors in the front of the bays opened out onto the track area, which looked onto a big berm behind Pitstop Row.

The Hardys' bay was one of the last in the line, and fairly close to one of the big bends in the motocross course. A tall line of piled-up earth separated their garage from the track. The earth wall also cut down on noise from the course.

The garage area was noisy enough on its own, with all the racers working on their machines. Most riders left the big doors of their bays open; the tiny, metal-cased garages got too warm with the doors shut.

Jamal had to run in the first race of the day, so he headed out while the Hardys were still working on their preparations. Frank and Joe had decided to rig small short-range radios in their helmets so they could talk to each other during the races. Paco Fernandez stopped by and handed the brothers their assignment sheets for the day.

As the Hardys wheeled their bikes out toward the track, Jamal returned. He was covered from head to toe with mud, so much so that you could hardly recognize his black and red uniform. Despite the mess, he wore a grin from ear to ear. "First in my heat," he said. "I'm on to the next round—and a good spot for tomorrow's Enduro."

"We've caught a tough break," Joe said, frowning. "Both Frank and I are competing in the same heat."

"Plus, we're up against Amber Hawk," Frank noted, checking their starting papers. "That'll make it harder to move on."

"Don't worry about Hawk," Jamal advised. "She has just as much chance to wipe out as anyone else."

Joe arched one blond eyebrow at his friend. "Do you really believe Hawk will wipe out, Jamal?"

Jamal laughed. "No, but it might help you if *you* believe it," he said.

The brothers laughed as well.

"Remember," Jamal said, "the top four finishers in each heat move on, scoring more points."

"Our strong suit is cross-country," Frank said. "It's the most like the riding that Joe and I usually do. If we can just hang on today, maybe we can pull something off tomorrow."

"Well, good luck," Jamal said. "Your race is about to start. I'll meet you trackside after you're done."

"Sure thing," Joe said. He and Frank wheeled their bikes out, down to Pitstop Row. There they made the final adjustments to their cycles while the previous heat finished. Surprisingly, Elizabeth Navarro finished first in her group.

"She must be better at this than she was at the Mixed Freestyle," Frank said.

"Actually, she did okay there, too," Joe replied. "I checked the standings and it looks like she had a strong finish after a shaky start."

"Maybe she was just nervous early on," Frank suggested.

The brothers fastened their helmets and rode their bikes to the starting line. They took their positions for the start, and waited for the Klaxon to sound and the flag to fall. The course had been toned down from the previous day, with the whoopdedoos resembling very tall speed bumps rather than high ski jumps.

At the blare of the buzzer the whole pack shot off the line. Amber Hawk took an early lead, but Joe and Frank stayed right behind her.

They hit the first whoopdedoo and arced over it, trying to control their airtime. "You can't accelerate when you're airborne," they'd once heard Jamal say. Back on the ground quickly, they raced side by side, both brothers hitting the throttle as hard as they dared.

Hawk landed in front of them, but skidded slightly as she did. The brothers started to catch up to her. Frank and Joe flashed each other a quick grin. The raw power and control aspects of this dirt-track race suited them much better than the Mixed Freestyle had.

The Hardys roared up the second berm, their tires spitting out dirt behind them.

Hawk regained control of her bike at the top of the hill, but the brothers caught up to her. They all leaped over the whoopdedoo side by side. The three of them landed simultaneously, with Joe and Frank on the inside lanes.

Suddenly, Hawk cut to the left, right in front of the Hardys' machines. Her tires hit a puddle and kicked a spray of mud up into the brothers' faceplates. She accelerated and darted in front of them.

Joe and Frank braked hard, barely able to see through the muck. They swerved farther toward the inside of the track as all three racers headed for a spectacular crash.

8 Wiped Out

Frank and Joe twisted their bikes sideways, trying not to ram into Hawk's yellow and green motorcycle. Amber flashed past them, her bird insignia a blur in front of their fenders.

Joe's back wheel hit a muddy spot and went out from under him. He skidded toward Frank.

Frank turned the handlebars over hard, causing his blue and white cycle to spin sideways. His back wheel missed Joe's head by inches as the younger Hardy went down into the dirt.

Joe skidded to the side of the track and piled into the hay bales stacked on the inside edge. Mud and straw sailed into the air with the impact, and Joe lay still.

"Joe!" Frank screamed as he fought to control his

cycle. He swerved in a crazy S shape, trying not go down. His bike's tires refused to purchase on the slick mud.

The remaining racers whizzed past Frank as he fought for control. In the next second he spotted Joe, lying trackside amid the dust. A chill shot down Frank's spine as he realized that he was headed right toward his brother.

The elder Hardy steered into the skid, but that just sent him faster in Joe's direction. Joe looked up, dazed, and saw Frank's bike coming at him. Frank laid the bike down, hoping he could stop in time.

At the last instant, Joe dove aside. Frank and his motorcycle brushed past him and skidded to a stop against the remaining hay bales.

Angry and covered with mud, Joe leaped to his feet.

"Are you okay?" Frank asked, picking up his bike.

But Joe had already hopped back onto his cycle. "Let's go!" he cried. He gunned his bike's throttle and rejoined the race.

The crowd in the grandstand roared their approval as Frank did the same.

The two of them rocketed around the next berm, but they had fallen far behind the rest of the pack.

"Keep at it!" Frank shouted into his helmet mike. "There's still a long way to go."

"We can catch up," Joe agreed. "I won't let Hawk beat us after what she did!"

They pressed forward as fast as they dared. Over the next few laps they made up much of the ground they'd lost. One by one, the brothers passed the other racers. But no matter how hard they tried, neither Hardy could catch up to Amber Hawk.

She crossed the finish line a good ten seconds ahead of Frank, who barely edged out Joe for second place. The two of them skidded their bikes to a stop at the edge of Pitstop Row.

Hawk wasn't waiting around to congratulate them. She waved perfunctorily to the crowd, then quickly headed back to her private garage bay.

Joe grumbled. "We could have finished *first* if it wasn't for her!"

"We're lucky to have finished at all," Frank replied. "These heats are tough, and placing in the top four is pretty good. We've made it through to the next round, and that's what really matters. How do you feel?"

Joe examined his mud-covered armor and battered bike. "I feel okay," he said. "The cycle seems good to go, too—aside from the mud."

"We can wash it down before our next run," Frank said.

"You might want to wash yourselves down, too!" jibed a friendly voice.

The brothers turned as Jamal walked toward

them. "Unless you don't care that no one knows it's you under all that mud," he continued. "Personally, when I win a race, I want the whole world to know it's Jamal Hawkins." He smiled, even though he was still covered with mud.

"You still look like the Amazing Muck Man to me," Joe said.

"I was just on my way back to the garage to change," Jamal replied. "I cleaned the bike up first. But I promised you guys I'd meet you trackside. How long until your next heat?"

"We're going to check right now," Frank said.

"Okay," Jamal said. "I'm on in a few minutes. Try to catch my next race, if you can. I've got to go clean up."

"See you soon," Joe said.

The brothers wheeled their bikes to the postrace information pavilion while Jamal went back to get his motorcycle and change armor.

Much to the Hardys' relief, their second heats didn't include each other.

"I understand now why all those Hayday girls aren't competing," Joe said. "Racing against your family is tough."

"We may still have to face each other in the finals," Frank said.

"I'll see you guys there," Jules Kendallson said, butting in. He stepped out of a crowd of racers gathered trackside to watch the heats the Hardys weren't participating in. "I saw you race," he said. "Nice recovery. You two are pretty quick."

"Yeah, thanks," Joe said. Noting that Kendallson's armor was clean, he added, "Good luck in your first heat."

Kendallson nodded and popped his black and green helmet onto his shaggy head. "Catch you in the finals." He pushed his green and black motorcycle toward the track and quickly disappeared into the throng of contestants.

As he left, Elizabeth Navarro pushed her yellow and white bike in the brothers' direction. "Fraternizing with the enemy?" she asked.

"Enemy?" Frank replied.

"You know," Elizabeth said, "the competition."

"Oh, you mean Kendallson?" Joe said.

"What was he trying to do?" she asked. "Psych you out?"

"No," Frank said. "He was just wishing us luck in the upcoming heats."

Elizabeth frowned and crinkled her nose. "That's odd," she said. "He hasn't been very nice to me."

"Maybe that's because you're ahead of him in the standings," Joe suggested. "Frank and I are in the middle of the pack, but you've been doing pretty well for yourself. He's probably jealous."

She blushed slightly. "Maybe. I've worked hard to get where I am," she said. "I've been riding a motorbike nearly all my life."

"Did your dad get you into it?" Frank asked. "We heard he used to ride a bit."

"Mostly I developed the interest on my own," she said. "My dad's been helpful . . . sometimes. Other times . . ." She sighed. "It's like he's living out his dreams through me."

Frank nodded. "That happens between a lot of parents and kids."

Elizabeth sighed. "That doesn't make it any easier," she said. "I think my dad wants me to win this particular race more than I want to win it myself. He even upgraded my motorcycle."

"It's a beautiful bike," Frank said, admiring the sleek white and yellow machine.

"Not that I don't want to win," Elizabeth said. Her blue eyes became steely at the thought. "I intend to beat everyone on the course—including both of you. I'm right behind your friend in the standings."

"You mean Jamal?" Joe asked. He checked his updates sheet. "So you are. Good luck with that."

"You don't really mean that," she scoffed.

Frank and Joe laughed. "Well, it wouldn't hurt to have Jamal taken down a peg or two," Joe said. "His confidence is a bit much! Good luck."

"Good luck to you, too," she said. "See you." With that, she wheeled her bike toward the track.

"Do you think she has a chance?" Joe asked.

"That's just what I've been wondering," said an older man's voice. Asa Goldberg pushed out of the crowd toward the Hardys. He stepped carefully between the muddy ruts beside the course so as not to soil his nice leather shoes. "The betting line on Navarro is pretty active."

"People are betting on this race?" Frank said.

"In Vegas, they bet on anything," Goldberg said. "I have people out there who wire me the odds. I can't decide who I want to back. The line's pretty good on you boys, too."

"Is that ethical for a sponsor?" Joe asked.

Goldberg shrugged. "I don't see why not. It doesn't change the money I'm putting up for the competition," he said. "Besides, having a stake in a race can make watching it more interesting."

"I thought the thrill of the competition was enough," Joe said.

"Maybe if you're actually *in* the race," Goldberg said. "But for folks like me, this benefit is a lot of standing around and glad-handing."

"I'm sure the Fernandezes can find some work for you if you want to volunteer," Frank said.

Goldberg gave a look of mock horror. "And get my hands dirty?" he asked, examining his fingernails. "I got out of that game a long time ago. If you don't mind, I'll leave the muddy work to you volunteers."

"Thanks," Joe said, not really meaning it.

"Well, I gotta be checking out the rest of the competition," Goldberg said. "Y'all race good now, y'hear?"

"We will," Frank said. Goldberg ducked back into the crowd once more.

"What do you think?" Joe asked after he'd gone. "Will he be betting on us?"

"I doubt it," Frank said. "We didn't give him any info to go on. Hey, there's Jamal."

Their friend, smartly dressed in new clean black and red armor, was pushing his motorcycle toward the track starting line. He had his helmet on and looked ready to go.

"Hey, Jamal!" Joe said, waving.

Jamal nodded in their direction, but kept going.

"He must have his game face on," Joe said.

"Let's watch the start of his race," Frank said, "before we start prepping for our next heat."

"Good idea," Joe said. The two of them pushed their motorcycles trackside, where they had a good view of the starting line. Jamal pulled his red and black bike up with the rest of the racers. Elizabeth Navarro was in the pack along with a half-dozen other riders.

The starter gave the signal, and all of the bikes roared off the line. Jamal got off to a good start. He took the jumps cautiously and accelerated smoothly over the whole course. He'd soon built up a decent lead on the rest of the field.

"Go, Jamal, go!" the brothers shouted as their friend's bike whipped past.

On the second lap, Jamal began having trouble.

He slipped on three whoopdedoos and took several turns too wide. The other racers began to catch up.

Elizabeth Navarro challenged him on the third lap. This seemed to make Jamal nervous. His slips became more frequent, and he nearly went down twice. Near the big U-turn, his tires almost brushed the hay-bale crash walls.

"I can't stand to watch anymore," Joe said. "Too intense! I'm going back to the garage to get ready."

Frank shook his head. "I don't know what's up with Jamal. He seemed to have it together for the first lap, but now he's falling apart."

Navarro took the lead, with Jamal well back in the pack.

"I won't give up on him," Frank said. "Win or lose, I'll see the race through to the end."

"Yeah, okay," Joe said. "Cheer him on for me. I'll see you back in the tune-up bay."

Frank nodded as Joe pushed his bike away from the track and back toward the row of small metal garages.

Joe felt disappointed that Jamal wasn't doing better. He'd hoped that all of them might secure a place in the motocross finals later that day. He let out a long sigh as he unlocked their unit and slid the folding metal door up into the ceiling.

As he did so, a muffled sound caught his attention.

Joe looked around. The small bay was dark all

the way to the door that led to the connecting corridor in back. Something near the workbench in the rear corner caught his attention As he drew closer, he saw it was a person lying on the floor.

Joe propped up his bike, picked up a nearby tire wrench as a makeshift weapon, then moved cautiously toward the back corner.

Suddenly he recognized the figure lying there. "Jamal!"

9 Off Course

Jamal was lying on the floor in his underwear, bound and gagged like a victim in an old-time gangster movie.

Joe raced forward and knelt by his friend's side. He quickly untied the struggling teen and removed his gag. "Jamal, what happened?" he asked.

"I was changing, and somebody hit me from behind," Jamal said. He pointed to a rising welt on the back of his skull. "The next thing I knew, I was tied up and lying on the garage floor." He rubbed his head. "Why would anyone do a thing like that?"

"Someone wearing your armor is competing on the track, right this instant," Joe said, putting two and two together.

"Someone is pretending to be me and is racing in my heat?" Jamal replied. He tried to get to his feet but staggered a little. Joe helped him up. "We've got to catch that guy!" Jamal said.

"We will," Joe said. "You okay?" Jamal nodded. "Then let's go. Hop onto the back of my bike."

Joe leaped into the saddle of his motorcycle and fired up the engine. Jamal pulled on a pair of sweatpants and hopped on behind him.

The two of them raced back to where Joe had left Frank. The elder Hardy did a double-take when he saw Jamal on the back of Joe's bike.

"If you're here," Frank said, "who's that riding your bike?"

"An imposter," Joe said. He swiftly angled his motorcycle toward the track.

"Joe, no!" Frank said, laying a hand on his brother's shoulder. "We have to tell the track officials," he said. "They can handle this."

"Right!" Jamal said. "I'll get the Fernandezes to stop the race. Riding the bike through the crowd would be dangerous. You two wait here." He hopped off Joe's bike, took a deep breath, and sprinted through the gathered racers toward the nearby Officials' Pavilion.

Meanwhile, Joe and Frank kept their eyes on the culprit. The imposter raced around the track, near the rear of the pack of riders.

"You think he's dogging it deliberately?" Frank asked. "He seemed to have the talent to do better, at first."

"I can't believe that we didn't notice it wasn't Jamal riding that bike!" Joe said angrily.

"I'm not surprised," Frank said. "With the body armor and helmet, it could be just about anyone on Jamal's cycle."

Joe scanned the racers competing in the heat. "You're right," he said. "From a distance, the armor and helmet cover up a lot of differences. You need the colors on the bikes and uniforms to tell the riders apart."

"That's why the fake Jamal only waved to us, rather than come over before the race," Frank said.

"I thought that was odd at the time," Joe said.

Frank mounted his bike and did a quick check of its systems.

"What are you doing?" Joe asked.

"Getting ready. Just in case," Frank said.

Jamal sprinted back and took a moment to catch his breath. Then he said, "They're going to put out the yellow flag, then stop the race and take custody of the imposter. The police are getting ready."

In the tower atop the reviewing stand, an official waved a yellow flag. Corri's voice boomed over the PA. "Sorry for the interruption, folks, but our finish-line system has developed a glitch. We don't want any errors calling the end of an exciting race. Please hold your positions while we solve the problem."

The crowd in the stands groaned, but the racers on the track slowed down in compliance with track rules. They held their positions relative to one another, waiting for the green flag to come out again.

The man wearing Jamal's armor looked around warily as the race ground to a near halt.

"He senses something's wrong," Joe said.

"He's probably worried that, at slow speed, someone might realize he's not Jamal," Frank said.

"Look!" Jamal said, pointing. "He's making a break for it!"

The imposter suddenly turned his bike around and headed for the north side of the course, where the track abutted the woods.

"He won't get away!" Joe said. He twisted his accelerator and shot forward. Frank did the same.

The two of them made several quick cuts between stacked bales of hay, and skidded out onto the track. They turned north, hoping to head off the imposter before he could reach the wooded trail.

The charlatan rocketed forward, soaring over the whoopdedoos at top speed.

"The jumps are slowing him down," Frank called to his brother over their headsets. "He's being careless."

"I don't think he's seen us yet," Joe replied.

They rode as fast as they could, keeping their airtime down when they hit the jumps to save precious seconds.

The imposter rounded the final turn before the trail into the woods, but the Hardys got there ahead of him. They screeched their bikes to a halt and positioned their motorcycles across the path, making it impossible for the man to get by.

Joe smiled. "It's the end of the line for you, bub," he said, knowing the charlatan couldn't hear him.

"Give up!" Frank shouted. "There's no way to escape."

In response, the imposter twisted his bike and zoomed east, off the track. He squeezed between several bales of hay and cut across the infield, a mass of ruts and wild grasses.

"Circle back the way we came!" Frank said. "We can cut him off there, too." He turned his bike around and looped back toward the eastern side of the course. Joe followed right behind.

The imposter bounded over the infield, dodging around scrub trees and other obstacles.

"This guy would do real well in the cross-country portion of the race," Joe called to Frank as they rode.

The elder Hardy nodded and pushed his machine faster. "He's going to beat us to the other side!" Frank radioed back angrily.

Sure enough, the imposter skidded his bike between two hay bales and back onto the southeast side of the track.

"He's in trouble," Joe said. "The authorities are waiting for him that way." The racetrack security guards and the Bayport police were already assembling on the south end of the track, near the finish line.

For a moment, it looked as though the imposter would run smack into them. But as he topped a big whoopdedoo near the fence, he suddenly swerved to the east. He soared off the jump, arcing high into the air. His back tire barely cleared the chain-link fence at the edge of the Fernandez property.

He hit the ground hard, almost fell, and had to lance his feet down to steady himself.

"That's one way to avoid the cops," Joe said. He and Frank raced to the same hill from which the imposter had just come.

"How'd he jump that far?" Joe said.

"We can make it too," Frank replied, "with a little assistance." He eyed a tall stack of hay bales between them and the fence. The distance from the top of the hill to the fence was longer, but the space between the mound and the bales looked like a very manageable jump.

Joe guessed his brother's plan and nodded his agreement. The two of them roared ahead, full-throttle.

They hit the top of the mounded earth and soared to the stacked bales of hay. The stack was six bales wide and deep, with plenty of room for a bounce landing and a second takeoff.

The haystacks shook under the Hardys as they hit. The brothers gunned their engines again and rocketed off. The chain-link fence stood lower than the bale stack, and both Hardys cleared it easily.

Frank skidded badly when he hit the grassy field on the other side of the fence and nearly fell. He touched down with both feet but kept going.

"How you doing, Joe?" Frank called as they rumbled over the field toward the industrial park.

"Fine," Joe replied. "Just jarred my bruised shins."

"Now mine are aching too," Frank radioed back. "Let's hope, that means that the imposter is feeling it as well."

The charlatan had a hundred-yard lead on them. That didn't seem like very much, but rows of giant pipes, laid horizontally, filled the industrial yard ahead.

"If we lose sight of him in those pipes, he'll give us the slip," Joe called.

Frank nodded. The two of them accelerated out of the weedy field and onto the surface of the pipe storage area, kicking up gravel on the way.

The man on Jamal's motorcycle turned left into one of the huge sewer ducts. The pipe was so large that he didn't even have to duck his head to enter.

Joe and Frank zipped into the pipe as well. A ring of sunshine at the far side illuminated their quarry.

The sound of the motorcycles in the cement tube was nearly deafening, but the brothers kept focused on their goal. The imposter exited the pipe and turned right, heading for another large opening.

The Hardys followed, just barely able to keep the man in sight. He turned right again, into the next pipe over.

"He could keep us running all day!" Joe said, shouting to be heard over the noise of the engines.

"Next time he zigs, you zag," Frank suggested. "With luck, we can catch him between us."

As they exited the big pipe, Frank followed the imposter, but Joe cut around the other way. The younger Hardy darted to the left, hoping to circle back in front of their foe.

Joe rode around the huge groups of pipes. He couldn't see either Frank or the charlatan, but he heard the echoes of their engines. He rounded a bend and came out near a chain-link fence at the far side of the property.

The imposter zoomed out of one of the big pipes in front of Joe. He turned away from the fence and drove straight toward the younger Hardy.

Joe smiled. The imposter's only way out was a small alley between the big rows of pipes. Just as the man in Jamal's clothes realized this, Frank roared out of the pipe behind him.

The charlatan gunned his accelerator and turned hard right. He zipped into the alley, with Joe in hot pursuit. The alley angled up, becoming some kind of loading ramp. It ran toward the back of the rows of big pipes.

"Stay there in case he gets past me!" Joe radioed to Frank.

The elder Hardy skidded to a stop at the alley entrance. He didn't see any other escape route, and he felt confident that his brother could handle the imposter.

At the end of the ramp, the charlatan turned left onto the tops of a row of big pipes. He deftly navigated Jamal's bike through the groove in between two pipes.

Joe gritted his teeth and turned after him. Though the route was very dangerous, he wasn't about to let the imposter get away.

The pipes ended abruptly in front of them. The man in Jamal's armor didn't stop; he accelerated. Before Joe realized what was happening, the imposter leaped his bike over the edge of the tubes.

Frank looked up as Jamal's bike sailed over his head. The charlatan soared over the chain-link fence at the edge of the property and landed, hard, on the other side. Again, he put his feet down to brace himself, but he didn't fall.

On top of the piping, Joe screeched to a halt, just

inches from the edge. "Rats!" he said. "There's no way I can make that jump!"

"Me neither," Frank called up to him.

Both brothers watched helplessly as the imposter rode across a field of weeds, then out onto a back road. In moments, he disappeared from sight.

The Hardys regrouped and returned, via the main road, to the Fernandez Cycle Track.

They found the police waiting for them at the main entrance. Jamal ran out as the Hardys got off their bikes to talk to the police.

"Did you catch him?" Jamal asked hopefully.

Both brothers shook their heads.

"The guy jumped a chain-link fence and got away," Joe said.

"Tell me he didn't jump the fence on my bike!" Jamal said forlornly.

"He did," Frank said. "We couldn't stop him. He took off down Lincoln Avenue, heading toward Kennedy," he added to the police.

Jamal's jaw hung open.

"You know what this means, don't you?" he said. "I'm out of the competition!"

10 Down & Out

Jamal paced the driveway like an angry lion. "I can't believe it!" he said. "First I get slugged, then my bike gets stolen, and now I'm out of the race! I had a shot at the top, but now I'm finished. Just like that!"

Neither Frank nor Joe knew what to say. Both brothers felt angry at having lost the imposter. Plus, they'd let down one of their best friends.

"Jamal, I'm sorry," Joe said.

"I know it's not your fault," Jamal replied, some of the anger seeping out of him. "It's just . . . I was doing so well!"

The police continued to search for clues around the track. Other officers left to pursue the man who had stolen Jamal's bike. "Well, at least you guys still have a second run," he said. "Let's go back to our repair bay and prep you for your heats."

Dejected, the three friends walked back toward their tiny garage.

"I don't mind getting beat," Jamal said. "I mean, I like winning and all, but losing is part of the game. Getting beat this way, though . . ." He sighed.

"Maybe this doesn't have to be your last race," said a voice from behind them.

All three teens turned and saw Trent Howard jogging in their direction.

"What do you mean, Mr. Howard?" Jamal asked.

"The rules say that competitors can't use different bikes during the race," Mr. Howard said.

"We're cooked, then," Joe said.

"Not necessarily," Mr. Howard replied. "I could replace Jamal's motorcycle with one of the exact same make and model. I have one in my collection."

"I doubt the organizers would go for that," Frank said.

"But they *might*," Jamal blurted. "It's worth a try! Thanks for the offer, Mr. Howard. Why don't you and I go talk to the Fernandezes about it."

"I'll be glad to, Jamal," Mr. Howard said. "There's just one thing. . . ."

"If it's money you want, I can't afford much," Jamal said. "But maybe I could rent the bike for a couple of days."

"I've got more money than I need," Mr. Howard

replied. "However, there is *something* that I want."

"The O'Sullivan SD5," Joe deduced.

Mr. Howard nodded. "That's right," he said. "I'd like to add the prize motorcycle to my collection. I will loan you a cycle identical to your own *if* you give me the SD5 when you win the race."

"That's a pretty steep price," Frank said.

Mr. Howard shrugged. "Take it or leave it."

Jamal frowned. "It seems I don't have much choice. Mr. Howard, you've got yourself a deal." He extended his hand, and they shook on it.

"Good," said Mr. Howard. "I'll have my lawyer draw up the papers deeding the bike to me, should you win. Now, let's convince the race officials to see things our way."

"Wait a minute," Joe said. "What if Jamal *doesn't* win the race?"

Mr. Howard shrugged again. "Then I've put a few miles on one of my motorcycles," he said.

"Okay," Jamal said. "Let's talk to Pops Fernandez before I change my mind." The two of them headed for the office while the Hardys returned to their garage to prep for the next race.

Twenty minutes later, Jamal returned to their small repair bay. "They went for it," he said, smiling. "That Howard guy is one fast talker. He even convinced them to let me run in the last heat of this round—so we have time to get the replacement bike from Howard's garage."

"Is it a long way?" Joe asked.

"Not far," Jamal replied. "But I'd better get going. See you back at the track." He turned and jogged off to meet Mr. Howard.

Frank watched their friend go. "Trent Howard gets a lot out of this deal," he said.

"He wouldn't be rich if he didn't have some business sense," Joe replied. "But I get what you mean. You think Mr. Howard could have set this up to get an angle on that prize."

"Hiring someone to take out a rider might make sense," Frank said.

"But why Jamal and not someone else?" Joe asked.

"Maybe because his bike matched one in Mr. Howard's collection."

"But could he be sure that the trick would be found out, and that the imposter would escape?" Joe asked.

Frank furrowed his brow. "You're right about that," he said. "And why would the charlatan ride badly during the race?"

"Maybe that was a ploy to call attention to himself," Joe said. He shook his head. "I don't know. There's a lot going on at this track that we don't understand."

"Like who broke into the office, and who tried to rob the gate money," Frank said.

"Did the same person do both?" Joe asked. "And if so, was it also the same guy who slugged Jamal?"

"All the culprits we've seen so far have worn motorcycle helmets and gear," Frank said. "Underneath a getup like that, it could be almost anyone—man *or* woman."

"Are you thinking it might be Amber Hawk?" Joe asked. "I wonder where she was during Jamal's race?"

"Maybe we can find out later," Frank said. "Right now, let's get down to the track. Your start time is coming up."

"And you're in the heat right after me," Joe added.

The brothers rode well in their next heats, each placing second—enough to move them into the final group.

Jamal rode even better, despite his borrowed red, white, and blue motorcycle. He placed first, with a very good qualifying time.

"I nearly beat Amber Hawk's mark," he told the brothers afterward. "If I'd just taken that last jump better . . ."

The brothers and Jamal ate a late lunch, then caught up with Corri for a brief chat before the final race. She was pleased with how things had gone that day. "Except for the trouble with the impersonator," she said. "Sorry about your bike, Jamal."

"I'm still hunting," he replied.

The lineup for the final race featured Amber Hawk, the Hardys, Jamal, Elizabeth Navarro, Paco Fernandez, Justin Davies, Marissa Hayday, Taylor

Fohr, and Sylvia Short. Aside from the Hardys and Jamal, the riders mostly avoided one another before the race. Paco Fernandez, being a goodwill ambassador for the benefit, worked his way from one contestant to the next, chatting pleasantly with each one. Only Amber Hawk refused to talk to him.

"Amber's not a very pleasant person," Joe noted.

"I get the feeling she's not here for the same reason that everyone else is," Frank said.

"You got that right," Jamal said. "I don't think she cares about Corri or her hospital bills. All Amber cares about is herself."

"There must be something else that interests her here," Joe said. "Maybe she wants that SD5."

"That could be," Frank mused. "Though only a few pieces of it are from Garth Metzger's garage, it's still one of a kind."

"That gives it enough cache for Trent Howard to want it," Joe said. "And maybe Hawk, too."

Jamal nodded. "Metzger was a big part of motocross history. What he did on the track made him a legend. Anyone here would be proud to have that bike."

"Too bad you had to give up your bid for it," Joe said.

"Hey, I'm happy to still be here, helping Corri out."

"So are we," Frank agreed. "Though if I could get one prize out of this contest, I'd settle for knowing who's behind the trouble at the track."

Paco dropped by, and the boys talked to him for a while, turning the conversation away from the mysterious goings-on to more casual subjects. As start time approached, the racers made their final preparations.

The Hayday sisters helped out Marissa. Jules Kendallson stopped by to lend Sylvia Short a hand. Paco had some of his local crew with him. Richard Navarro showed up to help his daughter, Elizabeth. And the Hardys assisted each other and Jamal.

Finally, they all took their starting positions on the well-worn dirt track.

With the sounds of the Klaxon, they shot off the line in a roar of engines and a cloud of dust. Elizabeth Navarro took an early lead, but Marissa Hayday soon passed her. The Hardys paced the leaders for a while. Then Jamal pulled ahead of his friends, and challenged Sylvia.

The two of them dueled atop the berms for a lap, chasing each other over the whoopdedoos and down the muddy slopes. The Hardys nearly caught up, but—even on a borrowed motorbike—Jamal had too much practice for them.

He passed Marissa and led the race for two laps. Then Amber Hawk made her move. She barreled past Jamal on the inside of a hairpin turn, then beat him over the top of the next whoopdedoo. The cloud of dust from her back wheel blinded Jamal momentarily, and Paco Fernandez passed him, too.

Justin Davies took a bad spill in the middle of the race and had to be carried away from the track on a stretcher. The hay bales piled by the side of the course saved him from serious injury.

Frank shot Joe a questioning look as they passed the scene of the crash. No one had been near Davies when he went down, and it seemed unlikely that anyone had interfered with him. The brothers were having no luck catching the leaders. "Face it," Joe called to Frank as they raced side by side on the course's longest straightaway, "we're just outclassed in this event."

"Keep at it!" Frank radioed back encouragingly. "Like Jamal said earlier, you can never tell when things might turn your way."

The teens ended up crossing the finish line in the middle of the pack, along with Elizabeth and Taylor Fohr. They were well ahead of Sylvia Short. Amber Hawk finished first, barely edging out Paco. Marissa came in behind the top two, with Jamal placing fourth.

"I'd have done better if I'd been on my own bike," he told the Hardys afterward. "On the other hand, I guess I should be happy to just be here." He smiled genuinely.

"Let's pick up the final placement sheet and see where we stand," Joe said. "I'm anxious to check my handicap for the Enduro."

"Me too," Frank agreed. "The woodlands should be kinder to Joe and me than this dirt track has been. Maybe we can make up for some lost time."

"After we do that," Jamal said, "we should get to modifying our bikes for tomorrow. The race starts at 8 A.M. That doesn't leave us a lot of time in the morning to get ready."

They picked up the sheet from the Officials' Pavilion, then decided to stop by the office.

"I want to thank Pops for letting me continue in the race," Jamal explained.

The three friends headed over to the old trailer on the east side of the property that served as the track's office. As they approached, they heard the sound of loud conversation drifting from the open window.

"I can't believe it!" a voice said. "You know what this means? If it's true, it could be the end of the benefit! It might be the end of the track, too," the voice continued. "This could ruin *everything* for us."

11 Endurance

"That sounds like Pops," Jamal whispered to his friends, listening to the conversation inside the main office. The Hardys nodded in agreement.

"Who do you think he's talking to?" Joe asked.

"I can't hear anyone else," Frank said. "Maybe he's on the phone."

"Should we listen in?" Jamal asked.

"I think we've heard enough," Joe said. He strode forward, knocked briefly, then hurried inside the trailer.

"I'll have to talk to you later," Pops said into the receiver, then hung up the phone.

"We couldn't help but overhear," Joe said as Frank and Jamal followed him inside. "What's going on?"

"Nothing to concern you, boys," Pops replied. "Just some track business."

"If it's about closing down the race, then I think it *is* our concern," Jamal said.

"Is this related to the other problems with the track?" Frank asked. "The attempted burglary in your office, the explosion of Henderson's motorcycle, the near-theft of the gate receipts, the impersonation of Jamal? These things look pretty suspicious when you put them all together."

"Really, boys, it's nothing," Pops replied. But his brave face was slipping.

"*Something*'s happening here," Joe pressed, "and it's putting both the competition and the competitors in danger. Who were you talking to on the phone? Why might it mean the end of the benefit? Mr. Fernandez, please tell us what's going on."

"Maybe we can help," Jamal added. "We don't want any trouble for Corrine, or your family."

Pops leaned against his desk and let out a long, low sigh. "Please don't go to the media with any of this," he said. "It really could be our ruin."

"We won't," Frank said. "And we'll try to keep the police out of it too."

"I was talking to Bob Ingersoll, my lawyer," Pops said. "He's just informed me that one of our sponsors is a dud. He doesn't have the money he's pretending to have."

"Who?" Joe asked.

"Asa Goldberg," Pops said. "He's as phony as that slight Texas accent of his. Goldberg's import company is deeply in debt. He's hoping publicity from this race series will boost his sales. That way, he can pay off his creditors, and keep his promise to us. If his sales don't rise, though . . ."

"Then he defaults on his part of the sponsorship package," Frank said, finishing the thought.

"Goldberg mentioned gambling to us," Joe said thoughtfully. "I wonder if that's how he got into debt."

"It doesn't matter," Pops said. He plopped heavily into a seat behind his paper-covered desk. "There's nothing we can do about it now. Without Goldberg coming through, we could end up deeper in debt than ever. We can only soldier on and hope that Goldberg's scheme works out. I'm not even sure that what he's doing is *illegal*—even if it is unethical. If the media learned about it, though, they'd shift their attention from the benefit to the scandal, and then . . ." He leaned his elbows on the desk and buried his head in his hands.

"Don't worry, Mr. Fernandez," Joe said, "we won't breathe a word of it to the media."

"I'm sorry that we barged in too," Frank continued. "We'd really only come to thank you for letting Jamal finish the race on his borrowed motorcycle."

"Don't thank me," Pops said wearily. "It was the decision of the rules committee. They're not associated with the race, and are only here to make sure the outcome is fair."

"Well, I'm sure you made a recommendation to them," Jamal said.

"As a matter of fact, I did," Pops replied.

"So, thanks," Jamal concluded.

"You're welcome, Jamal," Pops said.

"Don't worry, Mr. Fernandez," Joe said. "We'll help you figure out who's behind this trouble. We've solved cases like this before."

Pops thanked the boys, then stood and said good-bye. The Hardys and their friend returned to their garage bay.

"If Goldberg has gambling debts, he might be willing to do anything to pay them off," Joe said as they readied their bikes for tomorrow's Enduro.

"Whatever he owes money for," Frank said, "it's clear he benefits from added publicity at the race."

"Good publicity, or bad," Jamal added. "Like spectacular crashes, and robberies—"

"And the impersonation of one of the racers," Joe concluded.

"There's a lot going on here," Frank said, "We may not be able to sort it out right now, but before the race is over, we'll get to the bottom of this."

Tensions were already running high at the track by the time the Hardys and Jamal showed up the next morning for the final phase of the competition: the Enduro.

Riders and their teams busily prepared for the race, jacking up their bikes' suspensions, swapping out tires, and trying to optimize their engine performance for the cross-country leg of the challenge.

The Enduro would be hours long—by far the longest race of the benefit. The competitors would start at the dirt course, enter the woodland area to the north of the Fernandez compound, then run a circuitous route overland before ending up back at the raceway.

While the trails of the course were known to some of the local racers, the exact route had been kept secret during the previous two days of the race. Before the race, officials delivered a map of the course to the Hardys and the other riders.

"It looks like they've got big Day-Glo orange tags marking the course trail," Frank said.

"We've ridden through those woods before," Joe said. "That should give us an advantage."

"This will still be the toughest part of the race," Jamal told them. "The staggered start will make it tricky to catch up to the leaders."

"Harder for us than for you," Joe said. "You have an earlier start than we do, because you did better on the first two days."

"But we'll still have a chance to catch you once we get going," Frank said.

Jamal nodded. "The race is designed to give everyone a chance."

"That probably burns Amber Hawk up," Joe said. "She toasted the rest of us during the first two days of competition."

"Only because Ed Henderson was out of the race," Frank noted. "He'd have given her a run for her money if he hadn't gotten hurt."

"So, Hawk and Goldberg have benefited from the race's troubles so far," Jamal said. "Any more suspects?"

"Justin Davies had a grudge against you, but he's out of the picture," Frank said.

"There are still the folks that want that O'Sullivan SD5," Joe reminded them. "Trent Howard wants it badly enough to loan Jamal a replacement cycle. Someone else could be making a play for it too."

"Do you really think the bike could be what all this is about?" Jamal asked. "Even with the parts from Garth Metzger's garage, it's not worth that much. Mr. Howard told us that himself."

"I hope we can figure this out before anyone else gets hurt," Frank said. "Let's prep our bikes. Then we can scout our competition."

Joe chuckled. "And by 'competition,' my brother means *suspects*."

The other riders kept mostly to themselves as

they prepared for the race. Amber Hawk closed the doors to her private bay as she readied her motorcycle. The Hayday sisters worked animatedly on Marissa's bike. Richard Navarro showed up to help his daughter, Elizabeth, again. He was covered in grease and holding a wrench in his hand when the brothers walked by the Navarro bay. Taylor Fohr shared that space, but he wasn't talking to his garage-mates.

"You know, it'd be so much easier if villains wore symbols to make them stand out," Joe mused.

"You mean something like a skull-and-crossbones?" Frank asked, glancing at Elizabeth's helmet.

"Yeah. Like that. Of course, her yellow and white uniform detracts from the overall menacing effect." The younger Hardy smiled.

"So does her new motorcycle," Frank said. "If you're going to be a racing pirate, you really need a beat-up old bike."

"Like that one with the kick-starter that the prowler had," Joe concluded.

The brothers found Paco Fernandez near the race office, talking to Jules Kendallson. The two shook hands, though Paco looked somewhat disappointed. Kendallson wasn't dressed for riding. He was wearing cutoffs and a T-shirt. A new white bandage was wound around his forehead and another around his right knee.

"What's wrong?" Joe asked Paco.

"Jules and Sylvia are dropping out of the race," Paco said glumly. "We hate to see them go, especially at this late stage."

Frank frowned. "Why are you leaving, Jules?" he asked.

"Sylvia and I were out partying last night," Kendallson said. "We had a little wipeout, and got banged up." He pointed to the bandage on his head. "So Sylvia and I are taking the day off. We hate missing out on the prizes, but . . . well, we aren't in the top rankings anyway."

"What about your pledges?" Joe asked.

Kendallson scratched his head. "They'll come through," he said. "Hey, Paco, again, tell the rest of the family we're sorry." He turned and headed for the main gate.

Paco shook his head. "With Henderson and Davies out, and now these two plus a few more, the field is looking kind of thin. I just hope our sponsors don't see it that way."

"The top racers are still in the hunt, though," Frank said. "And you're one of them, aren't you?"

"I'm right behind Hawk," Paco replied. He forced a smile. "We're counting on everyone left to make this a really great and exciting race."

"No problem," Joe said.

Paco gazed toward the track. "You'd better get to your bikes—it's almost start time."

The brothers went back to the garage, where

they found Jamal finishing his preparations. The three of them rolled their bikes out to the course.

"I was thinking," Joe said to Frank as they went, "that Kendallson might not have gotten that leg injury last night. He could have hurt it making those jumps during the pipe factory chase."

Jamal nodded. "He wasn't in that heat, so he could have had time to clock me and be my replacement. We're about the same size."

"Size is hard to tell under the riding armor," Frank reminded them. "It really could have been just about anyone."

"But if Kendallson replaced Jamal, why did he do it?" Joe asked. "And how does his buddy Sylvia Short fit into the scheme?"

Frank shook his head. "I'm not sure," he said. "But all of us had better be careful during this phase of the race."

The contestants lined up in order of their placement: Those who had done best during the first two days of the race got a head start on the others; those with the lowest combined scores, would start later. Jamal was starting early, and Frank and Joe were placed in the middle pack.

"Welcome to the exciting final phase of the benefit challenge!" Corrine Fernandez's voice said over the loudspeaker. "Starting times will be staggered, according to each competitor's finish time during the previous two days. Everyone will race the course at the same time. The first racer over the finish line wins the competition—*and* the grand prize. Good luck, everyone! Here comes the starting signal for the first rider . . . GO!"

Amber Hawk roared off the line and around the dirt track, heading for the trail in the woods. Fifteen seconds later, Paco followed her; then, the others, according to their previous finish times.

The Hardys were starting in the first group, though well behind the leaders. They watched Elizabeth Navarro start, then Jamal.

"She looks a little shaky again today," Joe said about Navarro.

"I can't figure out what's up with her," Frank said. "One race she seems like a novice; then the next, an expert."

"Maybe she's got a bad case of nerves," Joe said. He nodded in the direction of Elizabeth's father, Richard. He was standing atop a nearby hill, fidgeting with a stopwatch.

Frank pulled his helmet on and checked the radio link. "Time to go," he said. He shot off the line, followed a few seconds later by Joe.

The two of them tooled around the dirt track before heading into the woods. The trees cut down visibility to either side, but they could still make out the other racers ahead of them.

Jamal had a good lead on the brothers, but Elizabeth Navarro had nearly caught up with him. Paco and Hawk also remained within sight. Even the top finishers seemed to be having some difficulty with the cross-country course.

Taylor Fohr rode between Navarro and the brothers. Frank and Joe took up positions nearly side by side—the way they traditionally rode together.

As they sped forward, Fohr began gaining on Navarro's shiny yellow and white 125.

Suddenly Navarro swerved, avoiding some obstacle in the trail that the Hardys couldn't see.

Fohr didn't spot it either. His front tire went into a deep rut in the road, and his back wheel skidded out from under him. He lost control of his bike and tumbled sideways, right in front of Frank and Joe.

12 Hidden Dangers

The Hardys hit the brakes as Fohr rolled toward their motorcycles. Fohr's bike spun like a top, throwing its rider off.

Frank and Joe swerved, both leaving the trail to avoid the falling cyclist and his machine.

Joe cut to the right, narrowly missing both Fohr's legs and the careening motorcycle. Frank cleared the spinning bike on the left, but headed for a stand of thick trees.

He cut the handlebars hard, and just avoided a big pine at the trailside. The elder Hardy skitted between several small saplings, their branches slapping against the side of his helmet.

Fohr rolled into the woods on the right side of the trail. His bike, badly damaged, crashed into a tree on the left. Fohr got up woozily; his riding armor saved him from serious injury. He got out a race-issued field phone and called for help.

In their rearview mirrors, Frank and Joe saw him get up. They both breathed a sigh of relief and steered back onto the trail.

"Watch out for that dip!" Frank called to Joe as they came up to the depression that had unseated Fohr.

The brothers whizzed past it, unscathed. "I don't know how Navarro saw that coming," Joe radioed back.

"Maybe we underestimated her skills in the woods," Frank said.

Trees flashed by as the cross-country trail wound deep into the heart of the forest. The brothers stuck close to each other—out of habit *and* because there seemed to be more safety in riding together.

"This has changed a lot since we last rode here," Joe said.

"I think we just missed this part of the trails," Frank called back.

He watched Navarro deftly dodge around the obstacles ahead of them. Though she wasn't the fastest racer in the pack, she was rapidly gaining on the leaders, who seemed to be having more trouble with the course.

"It looks like Navarro knows this trail real well," Joe noted.

Frank nodded. "She seemed shaky at first, but the way she's riding now, you'd never know it."

Another racer ahead of them went down, unseated by the trunk of a newly fallen sapling at the turn of a bend. Again, Navarro avoided the obstacle.

"She must have eyes like an eagle," Joe said. "No wonder this trail is slowing the top riders down. There are hidden dangers at every turn."

"Don't let her get too far ahead," Frank radioed back. "She can scout the land for us."

The trail looped left, then right, then cut back on itself. The brothers lost sight of Navarro more and more as stretches of clear road became less frequent.

The whir of a helicopter overhead made the Hardys glanced up.

"Covering the race, do you think?" Frank asked.

"Probably," Joe replied. "Look out!"

Frank ducked out of the way just in time as a thick, overhanging branch whizzed past his head. Joe ducked too, and the big tree limb scraped past his helmet.

"Someone could have lost a head on that!" Joe said angrily. "Why didn't they eliminate a hazard like that from the course?"

"The trail does seem pretty rough," Frank replied, "even for cross-country. It could be that most Enduros are like this, though. Jamal told us they were difficult."

"There's tough, and then there's *deadly*," Joe said.

"Well, let's make sure that this ride falls into the first category, rather than the second."

Joe barely heard his brother's reply. Something in the course seemed to be interfering with their radio transmissions.

In the next few minutes, they passed a couple of bikes by the side of the road. One had blown a tire, and the other had a bent front fork. The riders seemed uninjured, and both of them were talking on cell phones to race officials.

Frank and Joe glanced warily at each other; the course had claimed two more "victims."

The race leaders came into sight ahead of the brothers. Jamal and Elizabeth rode nearly side by side, dueling for third place. Hawk and Paco raced in front of them, still a good distance ahead. Marissa Hayday rode in fifth place, between the Hardys and the pack at the front.

"I don't know whether to be happy that the trail is slowing the leaders down, or worried about what might be coming next," Joe called to Frank.

Frank didn't hear him, though. He'd pulled ahead of his brother, temporarily out of radio range. Frank gunned his engine and headed for the leaders.

Joe bore down and accelerated as fast as he dared over the bumpy, irregular trail.

Soon the course widened out, and the trees fell

away for a moment. Jamal took advantage of the change and accelerated past Elizabeth, taking a clear hold on third place.

Marissa Hayday made a move too, closing in on Navarro's shiny motorcycle. Hayday swung out, heading for a stretch of wide, leaf-covered clearing, trying to loop around Navarro and Jamal, who were both sticking to the rocky trail.

Navarro braked when Hayday cut in front of her. But Hayday's wheels skidded on a slippery pile of leaves at the trail's edge. She fell, though not very hard. Elizabeth Navarro accelerated away from her. Frank and Joe zipped past Hayday as she picked herself and her bike out of the bracken.

A bump in the road sent Jamal into the air. He fought hard and managed to control the motorcycle as it came down. Navarro scooted sideways, avoiding the rock that had nearly unseated Jamal. She closed in and passed him. The two raced nose to tail for a while.

Following Elizabeth's course, both Frank and Joe avoided the bump.

The trail narrowed in again, forcing Jamal to abandon his attempt to pass Navarro as they went uphill. Ahead, Hawk and Paco dipped out of sight as they crested the rise.

Elizabeth and Jamal struggled up the slope as the course suddenly became mired with sand and gravel.

Frank saw his chance and took it. While Navarro and Jamal skidded on the loose earth, he cut to the right, up a rocky outcropping. With a surge of speed, he passed both his friend and the rider in yellow and white.

"Yeah! Go Frank!" Joe cried. Then his wheels caught on the same scree that had slowed the other two. He was too far behind to use the route that Frank had taken. He kept touching his feet down to steady himself.

Elizabeth's gleaming motorcycle climbed up on the rocks and surged forward once more. Jamal did the same, keeping close to Navarro's back tire. Joe kept plodding forward, kicking up a cloud of dust as he went.

Frank, Elizabeth, and Jamal disappeared over the top of the rise. Joe glanced back. No other racers were in sight; even Hayday had been lost from view. Joe knew that, if he was to have any chance, he couldn't let the distance between himself and the leaders get any larger.

He struggled up the hill until he could finally use the rocky path that Frank and the others had discovered. His bike's tires found better traction, and he zoomed up the wooded hill. As he reached the top, he saw Frank leading the others at the bottom of the next valley.

The woods opened out a little below. The trail widened only to narrow again as it headed toward the top of the next rise. Joe gunned his engine and shot downhill.

At the bottom of the decline, Jamal and Elizabeth jockeyed for position. As they reached the short straightaway before the next rise, a battered blue-gray motorcycle surged out of the woods toward them. Two people in cycling leathers rode on the back of the bike.

Jamal and Elizabeth didn't see the intruders zooming toward them. The gloved hand of the intruder riding on the back of the bike held a long, stout stick.

Joe watched in horror as the helmeted rider raised the log like a baseball bat. The intruder took aim on the unsuspecting Jamal.

"Jamal, look out!" Joe cried, knowing full well that his friend couldn't possibly hear him.

The intruder surged into Jamal and Elizabeth as they rode side by side across the narrow trail. Neither one of them saw their attacker coming.

The enemy bike roared into them from the side, like a wolf pouncing on unsuspecting deer. The rider on the back of the bike swung the big stick toward Navarro's midsection.

At the last second Elizabeth noticed the tree limb and turned her bike slightly. But Jamal was in the way, and the two of them bumped hard. The stick missed both of them, but Jamal's and Elizabeth's machines got tangled. They careened off the course and into a nearby clearing. Their bikes twisted around as they went, as though caught in a frantic dance. Jamal and Elizabeth fought to maintain control, but both bikes went down.

Jamal hit first, landing in a pile of leaves by the side of the clearing. His borrowed bike skidded to the ground beside him. Elizabeth sailed head over heels and landed hard at the base of a tree. Her shiny new bike kept going and smacked into a boulder protruding from the ground nearby.

Jamal rolled over and tried to stand; Elizabeth lay flat on her back, totally still.

13 Not Out of the Woods Yet

"You rats!" Joe cried as he raced downhill toward the scene of the ambush. "Frank! Frank, come back!"

No reply came from Joe's radio. His brother was too far up the next rise to hear him. Neither Frank nor the other leaders had noticed the attack in the valley below.

The thieves stopped their bike amid the fallen riders. The helmeted intruder in back got off their motorcycle, went over to Jamal, and kicked him in the chest. Jamal went down.

Joe charged down the slope and into the small clearing. The ambushers turned as they heard him coming, but they reacted too late. Joe stuck out his left arm, looking to clothesline the dismounted bandit.

The thief ducked and tried to bring up his big stick. Joe grabbed the lumber and jerked it out of the bandit's hand. The man lurched away as the younger Hardy swung the piece of wood at the ambusher's helmeted head.

The bandit who was still on the motorcycle surged forward. His front tire slammed into the side of Joe's bike, barely missing the younger Hardy's leg. Both intruders were about the same size as Joe; both wore identical black riding leathers and beat-up gray helmets.

Joe's bike skidded to a halt, and the impact jarred the piece of lumber from his hand. He kicked out at the intruder's motorcycle and caught the bandit's left thigh. The ambusher yelped and drove away from the younger Hardy.

The second intruder grabbed Jamal's motorcycle and started it up. As his partner circled around Joe, he grabbed the stick again and began to circle as well.

Joe and his bike stood caught between the circling bikers. Jamal, stunned, lay nearby, and Elizabeth still wasn't moving. With the bandits zooming around him, Joe had no good way to protect himself.

The biker with the tree limb laughed. "Looks like we may have even *more* bikes to add to our collection!" he said. The other bandit laughed as well. The bright, high tones in the voice told Joe that a woman lurked under that battered helmet.

"Just try it!" Joe cried. The man on Jamal's

borrowed cycle raised the stick and came in on the unarmed teen. Joe braced himself for the impact.

"Joe, duck!" Frank's cry crackled over Joe's helmet radio.

Joe ducked. Out of the corner of his eye he spotted Frank's motorcycle running up the back of a nearby boulder.

Frank's bike soared through the air, right at the log-wielding ambusher. The bandit turned, but not in time. Frank soared high over Joe's bike. His back wheel clipped the bandit's helmet on the way past.

The ambusher with the tree limb toppled sideways, off Jamal's borrowed bike. He hit the ground hard, and the bike crashed into a nearby tree.

Joe gunned his throttle and surged toward the startled second intruder. His front wheel hit her machine just in front of the engine, barely missing the woman's leg.

The woman pitched sideways, and her bike landed on top of her, pinning her to a pile of leaves. Neither she nor the man with the stick got up.

Joe and Frank got off their bikes.

"Man, am I glad you showed up," Joe said to his brother.

"I just happened to look back at the top of the next ridge," Frank said. "I spotted the trouble and turned back to help."

"We're lucky you did, or all three of us would have been toast," Joe said.

The Hardys stripped off their belts and tied the ambushers' hands with them. Then they went to see about their friends.

"I'm okay," Jamal said woozily. "Did you get the number of the train that hit me?"

"We got *their* numbers, all right," Joe said. "Whoever they are, they'll have a lot of explaining to do down at the police station. How's Elizabeth, Frank?"

The elder Hardy shook his head. "She's pretty badly hurt," he said. "She's babbling, not making much sense."

Joe and Jamal gathered around the injured teen. She looked up at them with her big blue eyes, but didn't seem to see them. "Watch the mud on the upslopes," she said. "They won't be expecting that . . . make sure . . . whatever you do . . . make it past the bridge first . . . home free, then. All the way to the winners' circle . . . make it past the bridge first. . . ."

"Is there anything we can do?" Joe asked.

"Let's call for help," Frank said. He pulled out his race-issued field phone and dialed the authorities. He relayed the information about Elizabeth's injury and their location, then hung up. "That's it," he said. "There's nothing more we can do but keep her comfortable and wait."

"Well, I want to see who these bandits are," Joe said. "They've caused an awful lot of trouble during this race."

Jamal glared at them. "You can say that again. Look at the bike Mr. Howard loaned me! It's a mess! There's no way I can finish the race now, and it's all because of these goons."

Frank and Joe knelt beside their unconscious prisoners and removed the bandits' helmets.

"Jules Kendallson and Sylvia Short," Frank said, not sounding too surprised.

"I thought they seemed a bit out of their league in this competition," Joe said. "Now we know why."

"These guys only entered the race to steal?" Jamal asked.

"That's about the size of it," Frank said. "It looks like they faked their injuries to get out of the final day of the competition. I thought Jules's blood-stained bandage seemed a little . . . convenient. These two could definitely have been behind the robbery attempts at the raceway."

"Before you showed up, Frank, they said something about having even *more* bikes to add to their collection," Joe said. "At the time, I thought it might have been Trent Howard under one of those helmets. But I guess these two were just planning to stealing motorcycles for profit."

"That makes sense," Frank said. "Jamal's bike was a collectible, and Elizabeth's was practically new."

"The police will deal with these guys now," Joe said. "After this stunt, they won't be doing any more stealing for a long time."

"It looks like I won't be stealing any wins, either," Jamal said forlornly, "even if the cops find my original bike now. But that doesn't mean you guys have to quit. Someone needs to stay with Elizabeth, and since my bike is messed up, it might as well be me."

As the friends talked, several racers had zoomed past the clearing on the nearby trail. Until that moment, neither Hardy had even considered getting back into the race. Frank and Joe looked at each other, torn between staying with their friend and finishing the Enduro.

"Look," Jamal said, "if none of us finishes, then it's like these goons have achieved some kind of victory. Don't give them that satisfaction. I'm sure the rescue copter is on the way. Get back into the race and try to win. Do it for me and for Elizabeth, and for all the others they messed with. Most of all, though, do it for Corri."

Joe and Frank slowly nodded. "Yeah, okay," Joe said. "When you put it that way . . ."

He and Frank got back on their bikes and started the engines. With one last glance at Jamal and Elizabeth, they headed back to the trail and rejoined the race.

They'd lost a lot of time during the ambush. And as they raced through the woods, the idea of catching any of the leaders seemed pretty hopeless. Despite that, both brothers remained determined to finish the race.

As they went, they passed two riders who had passed them during the ambush. Their bikes were mired in mud just above the bottom of steep hills.

The Hardys went around them and kept pressing forward. Marissa Hayday waved to the brothers as they passed her—she'd fallen victim to a mud slick as well. As Frank and Joe reached the top of the next rise, they spotted the leaders once more.

"They must have had some real trouble," Joe called to Frank.

"Look at the mud on their uniforms," Frank replied. "I think Paco and Hawk got stuck too."

Mud covered both the leaders and their bikes.

"Lucky for us that Hayday and the rest got stuck first, otherwise we might have hit that muck as well," Joe said.

"Luck or not, we have a chance to catch up," Frank said. He twisted his throttle to full speed and rocketed downhill. Joe did the same.

Below, the trail leveled out as it approached an old wooden bridge spanning a ravine. The gulch was only about forty feet deep, but there didn't seem to be any other way across it besides the bridge. Parts of the railing had fallen off, but the bridge otherwise seemed in fairly good repair. Its stout, wooden legs reached down the side of the adjoining hills, into the stream bed at the bottom of the defile.

The brothers reached the bridge just as Paco and Hawk raced off the other side.

The span was fifty yards wide, and too narrow for more than one bike to cross at a time. Frank went first, with Joe following right on his fender. The slats of the old bridge creaked and clattered as the brothers zoomed over them. They reduced their speed a bit to make sure they didn't fall off the sides.

"It's a long way down," Joe said as they crossed, eyeing one of the spots where the bridge's railing had rotted away.

Just as he said it, the span suddenly lurched under them.

"Look out!" Frank cried. "The bridge is collapsing!"

14 A Long Way Down

"Keep going!" Joe called. "It's our only chance!"

He and Frank barreled ahead full throttle. The bridge's timbers continued to groan. Suddenly, the span broke.

Ancient boards toppled off the trestle near the far side of the gorge. Shards of wood tumbled down the slope and landed in the stream far below.

"Jump for it!" Frank shouted.

He and Joe both angled for a break in the rail.

They soared through it, one after another, just as the bridge broke away beneath them. With a final snap, the aged structure twisted and toppled toward the stream below. The ground shook with a thundering crash as the entire span landed at the bottom of the ravine.

Joe and Frank hit the far side of the gorge just below the top of the muddy slope. The incline ahead of them was steep, but no steeper than parts of the trail had been before.

Their wheels spun and kicked dirt into the air. The brothers pushed with their feet, but it didn't help much. The rim of the gorge, only a few yards above them, seemed miles away.

"Don't give up!" Frank cried.

"Like I intended to fall down this hill?" Joe shot back.

Twisting their throttles full open, they surged up the slope. They barely stayed upright, but they reached the top. Both brothers paused at the edge, caught their breath, and looked at the wreckage below.

"That could have been us," Joe said.

Frank nodded. "It's lucky no one else was on the bridge when it collapsed. Someone could have been killed here."

"There have been a lot of places like that on the course," Joe said. "And much of the time, the folks who could have been killed were us."

"You're not suggesting that the Fernandezes laid out the course to thin the competition?" Frank said.

"I know, unlikely," Joe replied. "But this definitely seems out-of-bounds, even for an Enduro race." He twisted his throttle and shot down the trail once more. Frank followed behind.

They went as fast as they could but only caught a glimpse of the leaders ahead of them. As they came out of the woods, back onto the dirt raceway at the Fernandez Cycle Track, they spotted Paco and Hawk streaking toward the finish line.

The two battled head-to-head around the curves and over the whoopdedoos, then roared toward the final straightaway. At the last second, Paco surged forward, beating Amber Hawk by inches. The crowd in the grandstand went wild. Corrine Fernandez's voice boomed over the PA system: "And it's Fernandez by a nose! Paco wins! Paco wins!"

Each of the brothers smiled beneath his helmet, but they still had most of a lap to complete. The Hardys dueled side by side, going as fast as they could. Their arduous trek had tired them both, but neither was willing to admit defeat.

They glanced briefly at each other as they flashed over the finish line. Exhausted, both brothers skidded to a halt.

"Who came in third?" Joe asked, pulling off his helmet. "You or me?"

Frank shrugged and pulled off his helmet as well.

"A tie!" Corri's voice said over the loudspeakers. "A tie for third between Joe and Frank Hardy!"

Frank slapped his brother on the shoulder.

"Well, that was satisfying," he said. Joe smiled and laughed. The crowd that had assembled beside the raceway surged around them as they wheeled their bikes off the track.

The race officials ushered the Hardys to the Winners' Circle, an area just below a special grandstand stage set up for the awards ceremony. The stage was six feet tall, with a curtained-off area at the back. The Winners' Circle stood to the left of the platform. There, the brothers joined Paco and a very angry-looking Amber Hawk. "This is favoritism!" she complained. "It's all a plot to avoid giving away the prizes!"

"Do you think she could be right?" Joe whispered to Frank. "Could the Fernandez family have set all this up, just to get more money for themselves?"

"I'm hoping that Jules and Sylvia were the only criminals involved with the race," he replied. "But let's see how all this plays out."

Pops Fernandez came down from the announcer's tower to preside over the certification of the race results. "Now, now," he said, grinning from ear to ear. "No need to get upset. This race series is being presided over by official, impartial judges from the Northeastern Motocross Circuit. There will be no favoritism in our results." He smiled again for the cameras that crowded around the winners.

Amber Hawk didn't look convinced. She scowled in the direction of the judges.

Pops talked to the race review committee while Amber Hawk fumed. Paco smiled broadly and shook hands as people congratulated him for winning the race. The media focused exclusively on the tension between Paco and Hawk, leaving the Hardys by themselves.

People milled around everywhere, trying to snatch up prime spots for viewing the awards ceremony. Many riders who hadn't finished the race had already made their way back to the compound. They joined the audience and sponsors, waiting for the awards to be handed out. Asa Goldberg and Trent Howard both stood in the crowd near the winners, beaming.

"Howard thinks he might have a shot at getting the SD5 from Paco," Frank surmised. "Goldberg looks pretty pleased too."

"This result played into their hands, all right," Joe said. "In fact, most everything in the race seems to have gone their way."

"Except for the damage to the motorcycle that Howard loaned Jamal," Frank noted.

"Would you give up a newer bike to gain a classic from the Metzger garage?" Joe asked rhetorically.

Frank sighed with exasperation. "With all the trouble during the race—especially the last leg—I don't see how there can really be an uncontested winner. No matter how it turns out, no one will be completely satisfied."

"No one except the Fernandezes," Joe said. "And maybe the cops. With the capture of Kendallson and Short, they can stamp this one 'Case Closed.'"

"Maybe," Frank said. "A couple of things are still bothering me, though. I was paying attention to the way Short and Kendallson raced."

"Me too," Joe said. "You always have to check out the competition."

"Did it seem to you that either of them had extraordinary riding skills?" Frank asked.

Joe shook his head. "Nope. They were pretty average. Short did okay in a couple of heats, but that seemed more luck than anything else. Even *she* seemed surprised by her success."

"That's what I thought too," Frank said. "But the biker we chased through the pipe yard was no amateur. He made some jumps that you and I couldn't even attempt. There are other things, too—like all the hazards on the Enduro."

"They were tough, all right," Joe said. "Elizabeth Navarro seemed to handle them okay. But the rest of us . . . If didn't know better, I'd think she almost knew what was coming. But how could that be? None of the contestants were allowed to ride the course before the race."

"Wait a minute . . . !" Frank said.

Before he could complete the thought, Pops Fernandez mounted the makeshift stage and took the microphone.

"Behind this curtain," Pops said, "is the O'Sullivan SD5—a reconstruction of a classic motorcycle, incorporating parts from the garage of the legendary motocross champion Garth Metzger." Mr. Fernandez smiled broadly. "This motorcycle will be awarded to the winner of the Corrine Fernandez Benefit Challenge. After some discussion, our impartial judges have decided to award first place to . . . Paco Fernandez! Come up here and accept the prize, Paco!"

Mr. Fernandez beamed as Paco left his bike in the Winners' Circle and mounted the stage. Amber Hawk growled and stalked off. A good portion of the media trailed in her wake.

"Thanks, Pops," Paco said. "But I don't know if I can accept this. I got in this race to help my sister, not to win a prize."

"Well, let's take a look at that SD5, anyway," Pops said. He motioned to some stagehands at the side of the platform, and they pulled the golden curtains open.

Atop the stage stood the beautifully restored O'Sullivan SD5. Its shining black and chrome-silver paint job glittered in the afternoon light.

And astride the cycle sat a man dressed in a black leather riding outfit. A black, visored helmet, emblazoned with a silver skull, covered his head.

As the curtains parted, everyone gasped as the rider gunned the motorcycle's engine and shot off the stage, straight toward the crowd.

15 The Great Plan

The spectators in front scattered as the O'Sullivan SD5 flew off the stage toward them.

The classic bike hit the ground and roared forward, heading for the motocross track. Pops, Paco, and the others who had gathered for the award ceremony stood stunned. "He's stealing the grand prize!" someone shouted.

Frank glanced at Joe. Both brothers hopped on their bikes and fired up the engines.

"Out of the way!" Frank called as the two of them rolled forward.

The crowd parted, and the Hardys rocketed toward the track, chasing the skull-helmeted bandit.

"I think that's the same guy we chased the other day," Joe said.

"With that jump off the stage, you can count on it," Frank replied.

The brothers skidded onto the dirt course as the bandit hit the top of the first berm. The thief raced across the course, heading toward the fence on the east side of the property.

"He's going toward the pipe yard again," Joe called.

"No," Frank replied. "He's angling toward the cement factory next to it. That's an easier jump to make."

The bandit zoomed up a nearby berm and soared easily over the chain-link fence onto the adjoining property.

"Easier for him . . . and for us!" Joe said. He sailed over the fence right behind the thief. Joe landed hard but stayed on his seat.

Frank landed behind him and to one side. The elder Hardy skidded and nearly fell off his bike. "Keep going!" he radioed to Joe.

The complex ahead of them was filled with huge piles of gravel and limestone, stacked like mountains in the factory yard. Because it was Sunday, the factory itself was closed. The towering ramps leading from the rock piles up to the big building weren't moving. No steam belched from the smokestacks perched atop the tall, flat-roofed building.

The bandit glanced back and saw Joe chasing him. Skull-Helmet veered to the right, circling around one of the big piles of gravel.

Frank righted himself and shot after the other two. Seeing the bandit's course, he circled the other way around the gravel pile. He hoped that, this time, he and Joe might catch the thief between them.

The brothers met on the far side of the pile, trapping the bandit on either side. Instead of surrendering, Skull-Helmet turned his bike up onto one of the huge gravel piles.

The tires of the O'Sullivan SD5 skidded, causing a mini-avalanche, but the bandit kept going. Frank and Joe charged upslope after him.

One of the factory's big conveyor belts touched the gravel pile near its apex. Skull-Helmet skidded off the gravel mountain and raced up the long conveyor platform toward the factory roof.

"This guy drives like a maniac," Joe grumbled as he and Frank balanced their motorcycles carefully across the narrow scaffold. Dust flew up from their wheels, threatening to blind them, but they made it to the roof without falling off.

The bandit wound between the smokestacks and circled the factory's big air-conditioner units. Once, it looked like he might sail off the edge of the roof, but he turned at the last minute.

The Hardys split up again to increase their chances of catching him.

Skull-Helmet veered precariously along the edge of the roof, squeezing between skylights and the sheer precipice. Joe followed closely behind. Frank swung wide, trying to cut the villain off.

A big cement storage silo loomed into view beyond the rooftop. Frank spotted a ramp near the tower, leading down from the roof to ground level once more. The bandit saw it too. He jumped the edge of the roof, landed on the ramp, and zoomed downward.

Joe was still squeezing his bike between ventilators and had fallen behind. Frank went after the bandit himself. He careened down the rickety rampway while Joe stopped his bike at the roof's edge, beside the tower.

The younger Hardy looked down. The ramp that the villain and Frank were on zigzagged down the side of the building before passing beneath the legs of the storage silo. At that point, the big pylons that held up the ramp straddled some kind of loading area.

Joe spotted a large pull-chain suspended in the air just a few feet off the roof. The chain ran down from the silo toward a hatch above the loading area at ground level.

As Skull-Helmet raced down the final ramp, Joe leaped off the roof. He grabbed the pull-chain, throwing all of his weight into it. The chain jerked down, opening the trapdoor at the bottom of the silo.

The bandit looked up as tons of silty cement dust cascaded down from the open hatchway, right in front of him. He slammed on his brakes and tried to turn, but he couldn't stop in time.

Crash!

The falling cement dust buried Skull-Helmet up to his armpits. He and his stolen motorcycle stopped dead.

Frank hit the brakes and avoided the smothering cloud. Dangling on the chain above, Joe gave a loud cheer. Then he shimmied down to ground level to join his brother.

Skull-Helmet coughed and sputtered, trying to get out from under the sandy pile of cement. Frank stepped forward and pulled off the villain's helmet.

"Richard Navarro," he said, "currently motorcycle-magazine writer and father to Elizabeth."

"And formerly a skilled motocross racer," Joe added.

"I suppose we should add 'master criminal' to his résumé as well," Frank concluded.

"*Former* master criminal," Joe corrected. "Now he's just another crook on his way to jail."

Navarro spit cement dust from his mouth and sneered at them. "I nearly made it," he said. "It was just rotten luck that you caught me."

"And rotten luck for your daughter that you involved *her* in your schemes," Joe said. "She's in the hospital, you know."

"I know, but there was nothing I could do about that," Navarro said. "I had to finish my plan."

"And steal the O'Sullivan," Joe said.

"But it's not actually the SD5 you want, is it?" Frank said. "You only want certain *parts* of the bike."

"The parts that came from Garth Metzger's garage," Joe added. "What do you want with them?"

"If you're so smart, why don't you tell me," Navarro snarled.

"We have a pretty good guess," Frank said, "but we'll know for sure once we—and the police— examine the bike that's half-buried with you." He took out his cell phone and called the cops.

After the police hauled Navarro to jail, the Hardys met with Jamal and the Fernandez family in the office of the Fernandez Cycle Track.

"One of the things that was so confusing about this case," Joe said, "was that there were *two* sets of criminals."

"Jules Kendallson and Sylvia Short were stealing at the same time that Navarro was scheming to get his hands on the SD5," Frank explained.

"So Kendallson and Short *weren't* working with Navarro?" Pops Fernandez asked.

"No," Joe said. "They didn't know anything about one another."

"Although the actions of each of them provided good cover for everyone," Frank added.

"So which group did which crime?" Jamal asked.

"Kendallson and Short set the fire at the kick-start party," Joe said. "They used the smoke as a distraction to do a bit of pickpocketing."

"The fire played into Navarro's hands as well," Frank added. "He took the opportunity to examine the O'Sullivan SD5—which he needed to do in order to confirm his theory about the bike."

"Which was . . . ?" Corrine asked.

"We'll get to that in a minute," Joe said. "Kendallson and Short were also responsible for the box-office robbery, and the ambush near the end of the race. Their motive was profit, pure and simple. They entered the competition hoping to win the big prize. When they saw that they didn't have a chance, they decided to make whatever money they could on the side."

"Which meant jumping me and Elizabeth Navarro in the woods to take our bikes," Jamal said.

"Right," said Frank.

"Which one of them tried to rob the box office?" Pops asked.

"That was Jules," Joe said.

Paco scratched his head. "But he was on the racecourse at the time, competing."

"It was a nearly perfect alibi," Joe said, "but what happened to Jamal later allowed us to figure that out. Kendallson and Short pulled a switch. They're about the same size as each other, so Short put on Kendallson's armor and impersonated him during the competition. That's why 'Kendallson' did better in that leg of the race. She was a better rider than he was."

"Though neither of them was good enough to be in the top group," Jamal noted.

"Richard Navarro was behind all the other trouble," Frank said. "His goal was to get his hands on the SD5—by whatever means necessary."

"What about Elizabeth?" Paco asked.

"We think she was just a pawn in his scheme," Joe said. "She knew that he desperately wanted her to win the race, but she didn't know why."

Frank picked up his brother's train of thought. "At first, Navarro hoped he might be able to coach Elizabeth to victory. But she was too erratic as a rider to count on to win. Her nerves often got the best of her, though she had quite a bit of skill. He bought her a new bike to increase her chances, but that still wasn't enough."

"So Navarro decided to take things into his own hands," Joe continued. "His experience in motocross racing served him well—and his role as a journalist was the perfect cover. If anyone found him poking around the speedway, he could just say he was working on a story. Or he could say he was helping his daughter."

"He rigged Ed Henderson's bike to explode," Frank explained. "He's also the one who mugged Jamal and took his place during the race. Both of those moves were designed to help Elizabeth in the final standings. Joe and I realized later that the imposter had to be a very good rider in order to execute the jumps that he used to escape us."

"If he was that good, he could have entered the race himself," Paco said.

"Navarro himself told us why he couldn't," Joe said. "He didn't have the stamina to compete in long races—like the Enduro phase of this challenge. That's why he needed Elizabeth's help. She's young and strong, and a pretty good rider to boot."

"But not good enough to win without his help," Frank said. "So he sabotaged Henderson, replaced Jamal, and laid out a series of obstacles on the Enduro course."

Joe nodded. "We wondered how Elizabeth saw those obstacles before anyone else did," he said. "At the time, we thought she was just a good cross-country rider. There was another explanation, though: Her dad had 'set up' the course, then made her memorize the hazards. She probably just thought he had ridden the course before and knew what to expect."

"Hey!" Jamal said. "That's what Elizabeth was babbling about after she got injured!"

"Right," Frank said. "She was running through the instructions her father had given her to avoid the hazards. We didn't make the connection until after the bridge collapsed. Remember, she said to make sure to be over the bridge *first*? That was because her dad had sabotaged the bridge so it would collapse after a few cycles had passed over it."

"As we were riding, the Enduro seemed more hazardous than it should have been," Joe said. "Cross-country is tough, but no one's supposed to get hurt in it. Navarro deliberately made the course dangerous."

"He used the information he found in Pops's office the night before the race to plan his schemes," Frank said.

"That bandit handling an old, kick-start bike turned out to be a clue," Joe said. "He started that bike so quickly because that was the type of motorcycle he had learned to ride on."

"All right," Corri said, "now we know who was responsible for most of the trouble at the event, and we know what he wanted—the SD5—but *why* did he want it so badly? Why risk his daughter's life, and put everyone else in the race in jeopardy?"

"It all comes back to the bike's origins," Frank

said. "Pops cobbled the cycle together using some O'Sullivan parts from the Metzger garage. What your dad didn't know was that *one* of those parts was a lot more valuable than it seemed."

"Navarro had written a lot of historical cycling articles," Joe continued. "In his research, he came across the story of the 'super-cycle' that Metzger had designed just before he died."

"But a fiery crash destroyed that prototype engine," Pops added. "Those plans were lost forever."

"Not forever," Frank said. "Even a genius like Metzger couldn't build an engine out of nothing. Remember the story? He jotted down the plans when he got the idea, then made blueprints from them."

"But the newspapers reported that Metzger had destroyed those blueprints once the bike was done," Paco said.

"He did, but what he didn't destroy—and what Navarro found out about in his research—was the *original sketch* those plans were based on," Joe said. "He discovered that Metzger, who was nearly broke at the time, didn't sketch the plans on paper—rather, he scratched the idea for the engine onto a motorcycle gas tank."

"Most people assumed that that tank had been destroyed along with the blueprints," Frank said. "But Navarro found out that *wasn't* the case. Being broke, Metzger couldn't afford to waste good motorcycle parts. So, he just painted over the gas tank for use later."

Jamal snapped his fingers. "But he died before he could reuse it, so the tank remained in his garage."

"Until Pops found it and put it into the restored SD5!" Corri concluded.

Frank and Joe folded their arms across their chests and smiled. "That's what made the SD5 so valuable to Navarro," Frank said.

"Just think," Joe said, "if you'd known about it, you could have paid off Corri's medical bills without any trouble. Those plans are worth a fortune."

Pops shook his head in disbelief. "I thought that gas tank was just a souvenir I picked up at auction."

"Boy," Paco said, "those plans sure caused a lot of trouble."

"But the troublemaker is behind bars now," said Joe, "for good."

Paco looked thoughtful for a moment. "Once we copy the plans off the tank, I think I'll donate the whole bike to raise money for a hospital."

"That's a great idea, son," Pops said. "We've raised enough money with the race to cover our bills. It would be good to give something back to the community."

"I doubt you folks will ever have to worry about money again," Joe said. He, Frank, and all the others smiled.

"Well," Pops said, "now that you've solved *our* problems, what are you Hardy boys up to next?"

Frank and Joe both shrugged.

"Who knows?" Frank said.

"A long vacation, maybe?" Joe added.

"Well, whatever comes next," Jamal said, "I hope you'll both be ready to rev up and race new criminals like you did here."

The brothers looked at each other, smiled, and, in unison, said, "Count on it!"